Praise for

My Vampire and I
Volume Four

With loads of intense passion, meddling friends, and the threat by an ongoing enemy "Bound by Blood" is sure to keep the readers attention to the end, it has also become my favorite J.P. Bowie book
~ *Rainbow Reviews*

Mr. Bowie has continued his *Vampire and I* series with this action packed and fast paced story. I love how the characters from the earlier books lives are continued and enrich the plot line... Thanks go to Mr. Bowie for another edition to an incredible series
~ *Fallen Angels Reviews*

J.P. has a way with characters and emotions that draw the reader in ~ *Author, Carol Lynne*

Total-E-Bound Publishing books from
J.P. Bowie:

My Vampire and I
My Vampire and I
My Vampire Lover
Duet in Blood
Blood Resurrection

The Set up

Ride Em Cowboy

Halloween Angel

Personal Trainers

The Officer and the Gentleman

Anthologies:

Fabulous Brits: Under the Law
Heatwave: Summer Bliss
Naughty Nooners: Lunches in Laguna
Christmas Spirits: A Present Christmas

MY VAMPIRE AND I
Volume Four

Bound in Blood

J.P. BOWIE

My Vampire and I: Volume Four
ISBN # 978-0-85715-061-5
©Copyright J.P. Bowie 2010
Cover Art by Lyn Taylor ©Copyright 2010
Interior text design by Claire Siemaszkiewicz
Total-E-Bound Publishing

BOUND IN BLOOD

Dedication

For everyone who loves a sexy vampire story, for Michele who works so hard at making my stories better, for Carol Lynne who gives me endless support – and for Phil, who puts up with me and my flights of foolish fancy.

Prologue

Madrid, Spain: 1635

With considerable interest and excitement, Count Enrique Galvez watched the young man who had just entered the Grand Salon of the Palazzo de Granada. Tall, wide shouldered, with a mane of dark, almost black hair, and dressed fashionably in a coat of dark-green silk, the man exuded confidence and finesse. He would have been a stand-out in any social gathering, but here, amongst Madrid's nobility and jaded elite, he was magnificent.

Galvez was quick to make himself known. As soon as the man had been announced as Señor Carlos Galeano and greeted by his host and hostess, Galvez hurried across the room to where he stood making polite conversation.

"Your servant, Señor Galeano." The count bowed slightly. "I am Count Galvez, and I bid you welcome."

Carlos stared at the handsome count appraisingly. He had heard of him, and what he had heard were reasons not to seek him out as a friend. Still, garbed in a fine suit of blood-red silk, his dark-blue eyes alive with humour and mischief, Galvez seemed a suitable choice with whom to spend a few minutes of amiable conversation.

"I am pleased to make your acquaintance, Count." Carlos returned Galvez's smile and bow. "Now, perhaps you can show me where I can quench my thirst."

"Indeed I can."

Galvez tucked his hand under Carlos' elbow and steered him across the crowded salon to where servants poured wine into large crystal goblets. Carlos could not help but notice the admiring stares he received from both men and women as they passed, nor the sometimes wary looks those same people cast upon his companion. Galvez picked up a goblet from one of the trays and handed it to Carlos with a quizzical lift of his left eyebrow.

"Red. Is it to your liking?"

"It is. *Salud*, Count."

"*Salud*." Galvez picked up another glass and, with a sultry smile, raised it. "To your health." His gaze locked on Carlos' golden-brown eyes. "And please call me Enrique. These endless formalities seem redundant nowadays."

The men sipped their wine then Carlos looked around the salon for a familiar face. "Ah, there she is," he said, relieved to see his cousin, the Lady Andorra, chatting with a group of dignitaries on the other side of the room.

Galvez frowned. "You know the Lady Andorra?"

"She is my cousin."

"Ah." Galvez looked at Carlos from under his lashes. "She shares your beauty—a pity she does not also share your charm."

Carlos stiffened with shock at the man's rudeness, but before he could utter the angry retort that sprang to his lips, the count chuckled and touched his arm. "The Lady Andorra does not care for me and makes no bones about it. I see her coming this way, so I shall leave you immediately, although temporarily, and avoid her ire." He turned on his heel and disappeared into the noisy throng.

Carlos watched with awe as his cousin glided across the floor towards him. The Lady Andorra was a woman of unsurpassed beauty. Regally tall, she wore a gown of some golden gossamer like material that shimmered and drifted about her body as though it were a part of her. Her pale creamy skin and startlingly large dark eyes under a luxurious fall of black-as-midnight hair made her the envy of every woman in the room and the object of lust for every man. But if these men and women had known Andorra's otherworldly beauty hid a dark secret, their envy and lust might have turned to sudden fear.

"Carlos, you have been here all of two minutes, and already, you have conversed with that charlatan, Galvez." Andorra's eyes held reproof mixed with concern. "The man is not a worthy companion for you."

"And good evening to you too, my cousin." Carlos lifted her cool hand to his lips. "May I say you look more beautiful than ever?"

"You may." Andorra melted under her cousin's charming smile. She tapped him gently on his chest with her fan. "But please beware of men like Galvez — and the company he keeps. The Comte d'Arcy is a friend of his."

"Who?"

"A degenerate who, it is rumoured, dabbles in the black arts."

Carlos shivered with mock fear. "Oh, then by all means I shall avoid their company. One should be very afraid of those who dabble in what does not exist."

He grinned, and Andorra tapped him again on the chest — this time harder. "Do not laugh at me, Carlos. Galvez and d'Arcy are reprehensible scoundrels and should be barred from attending these soirées. "

"My dear cousin, if you were to bar every scoundrel from attending, this room would be near to empty."

Andorra managed light laughter. "You may be right about that, Carlos, but there are scoundrels — and then there are men like Galvez and *d'Arcy*. Just be careful, is all I ask."

* * * *

If Carlos could only have foreseen the events that followed, events that would plunge himself and Andorra into a nightmare of blood and death, he might have taken her words more seriously. Several nights later, he was invited to dine with Galvez. The invitation he received said it was to be a small and intimate dinner party, and despite his cousin's disparagement of Galvez, he accepted. As the evening progressed, as far as Carlos was concerned, it turned out to be a very strange affair. Little food was served or eaten, yet copious amounts of wine were served. The Comte d'Arcy was there, Galvez of course, and three other gentlemen whose good looks and graceful movements fascinated Carlos — one in particular, a slender young man with mesmerising, luminous eyes of a colour Carlos could not quite place — sometimes ice blue, other times a silvery grey. He was introduced to Carlos as Sir Aubrey Gallant.

"Sir Aubrey is visiting us from England," Galvez gushed. "He is on his way to France with the Comte d'Arcy."

Carlos felt an almost immediate attraction towards Sir Aubrey, finding he could not tear his eyes from the young man's steady, sensual gaze. None of the other guests seemed to mind when he and Sir Aubrey retired alone to one of the many ante rooms in Galvez's sumptuous home. As though in a trance, Carlos found himself in Sir Aubrey's embrace, the smaller man gazing up into Carlos' eyes, his sensuous lips curled in a lascivious smile. Sir Aubrey's arms slid around Carlos' neck and pulled him down for a long, languorous kiss that had his head thrumming and his cock hardening so swiftly he thought for a moment he would ejaculate inside his breeches. Gasping, he tried to release himself from the embrace, but the slender man's strength was formidable, and Carlos felt his clothes being stripped from his body — but how? Sir

Aubrey's arms were still entwined around Carlos' neck.

They were now both naked, and Sir Aubrey lowered Carlos to the floor, his hands everywhere at once, stroking, caressing every part of Carlos' muscular torso, lips teasing and nibbling at his hot, fevered flesh. Sir Aubrey took Carlos' throbbing erection into his mouth, sucking on it greedily, his lips gliding up and down the hard, thick length, bringing Carlos a sweet torture he could not resist. He came in great, wrenching spasms, his semen flooding the other man's mouth, his body arching off the floor in a paroxysm of ecstasy.

Smiling with satisfaction, Sir Aubrey sat astride Carlos thighs. For a moment or two, he massaged the bigger man's heaving chest, his fingers gently teasing Carlos' nipples then, very slowly, he lowered his head, his lips nuzzling Carlos' throat.

The pain of the bite made Carlos start with surprise. "What are you doing?" he gasped, pushing against Sir Aubrey with all his might, trying to force the man's mouth away from his neck. But once again, Sir Aubrey showed incredible strength. He clung to Carlos like a leech, sucking the lifeblood from the wound he had inflicted on Carlos' neck. Carlos tried to cry out, but no sound came from his lips. His limbs lost all power to move, his eyes, staring up at the painted ceiling above him, blurred and dimmed. He was losing consciousness, and try as he might, he could not stop himself slipping away into the darkness that now surrounded him.

Sir Aubrey sat up and wiped his lips with the back of his hand. He stared down at the young man who lay unconscious between his pale, sinewy thighs and chuckled softy.

"A delicious brew," he murmured. He rose and dressed quickly, leaving Carlos alone in the room, naked and defenceless. Sir Aubrey smiled at the two young men waiting outside the door. "He is yours now. I left enough for you both to enjoy."

The two rushed into the room and gazed down at Carlos. "He is beautiful, is he not?" one whispered, dropping to his knees alongside Carlos' body. With his forefinger, he traced the musculature of Carlos' chest, circling each nipple before teasing them with his teeth.

"Hurry and drink," the other hissed. "The scent of his blood is driving me mad."

"Patience. We are not always fortunate enough to have such beauty laid before us." The vampire breathed in Carlos' masculine scent, licked his muscular torso, nuzzled at the head of his spent cock. His fangs bit deeply into the artery that pulsed beneath the skin covering Carlos' thigh. A shudder of delight ran through the vampire's body as he gulped at the rich, sweet blood that flowed over his tongue. Impatiently, the second vampire pushed his friend out of the way, eager to slake his thirst and savour the lifeblood of their victim.

* * * *

Carlos awoke, his mind dull, his vision still foggy and unfocused. He groaned as he tried to sit up. It was as though every vestige of his strength had been taken from him, and there was a deep throbbing ache in his neck and thigh. He rolled over onto this side, trying to remember where he was and what had taken place. After a few moments, he managed to sit up and realised he was naked, his clothes lying beside him in a crumpled heap. Groggily, he reached for his shirt and, with difficulty, slipped it over his head. He encountered stickiness, and gasped as he stared at the blood coating his fingers.

What had happened? Slowly, he began to remember. Sir Aubrey—the two of them here, kissing, making love—and then...? He recoiled in horror at the realisation. The man had bitten his neck. Sir Aubrey was a vampire—and the others? He struggled to his feet and, with a supreme effort, pulled on the rest of his clothes. He staggered to the door, what little remained of his strength beginning to fade. There was no one in the drawing room, the house seemed deserted. A gentle whinny greeted him as he exited the front door. His horse, Samson, still tethered, pawed the ground impatiently. He put one foot in the stirrup, but could not find the power to hoist himself into the saddle. He had to lead Samson to the steps so that he could mount him using the top step as leverage.

How he managed to stay astride his horse all the way to his cousin Andorra's mansion was something neither of them could believe. Andorra, on seeing the wound on his neck and his skin devoid of all colour, knew it was too late to simply imbue him with her blood. Carlos was dying and would not last the night without her taking extreme measures. Still, she would not do it without his permission. Her revelation caused Carlos to stare up at her with shock, his dark eyes reflecting the sudden fear her words had brought him. She held his hand as she explained what she could do to save him.

"You will die, my dear Carlos, but you will be reborn. I will be with you when you awaken to guide you into this new life." She kissed his forehead tenderly. "Do not be afraid, Carlos, just tell me if I should proceed. I would not do this against your will."

Carlos' grip tightened on the small, cool hand that held his. His body was failing, his mind slipping into darkness.

"Now Carlos…" Andorra's urgent whisper close to his ear, seemed to come from far away. Tears filled her eyes as she listened to his weak, almost inaudible consent then she did what had to be done in order that he might survive this night of horror.

"Close your eyes, my dear cousin," she murmured gently — and then, she struck.

Chapter One

Los Angeles, USA, Present day

Chris Jeffries knew he was being followed. Ever since he'd left the warm interior of the Xtasy Club he had been aware of the long, dark shadow that would sometimes fall against the wall just ahead of him and the soft pad of footsteps behind him. He didn't dare look around. Instead, he slipped his hand into his pocket and palmed the vial of pepper spray he kept there for just such an occasion as this. At the first touch of a hand on him, he'd be ready to give the bastard a face-full of pain. Chris wasn't tall. He worked out regularly and figured he could probably defend himself in a fight, but why chance getting beaten up and subsequently out of work when pepper spray and a hasty retreat was a much better plan?

He'd only been working at the Xtasy Club a week. He'd been hired to take care of the bookkeeping by

Lonnie Zielowski, the owner. Lonnie had thought at first when Chris showed up at the club that he'd come to audition as one of the go-go boys he'd advertised for along with the bookkeeping situation.

"Sweetheart," Lonnie had told him, taking in Chris' shaggy blond hair, blue-eyed gaze, and tight, slender body, his pectoral muscles nicely defined under the chest-hugging T-shirt he was wearing. "You could make a helluva lot more money dancin' here. What d'ya say?"

Chris had said no thanks but asked if the bookkeeping position was still available.

"It's available, and it's yours," Lonnie had replied, rolling his eyes in disbelief that his offer to make more money had been refused.

Chris had feared the worst, bracing himself for all the innuendo and ball-grabs he was sure his new boss was bound to try and wondering if he could stand it. But to his surprise, Lonnie had so far shown him only polite indifference — and piles of back-dated work for him to upload into the computer.

He'd experienced some lewd remarks from the patrons as he passed through the club on his way to the office, things like "Nice ass, bring it over here" but that he could live with, and besides, some of the guys who frequented the club were cute.

But none as cute as the guy he'd noticed earlier in the evening. Only 'cute' was entirely the wrong word to describe him. To say he would stand out in a crowd was putting it mildly. He was beautiful—*beyond* beautiful—yet in a totally masculine way. Tall, wide shouldered, with a mane of thick, black hair that had Chris' fingers itching to run through it, and a brooding gaze from eyes so dark and mysterious they had taken Chris' breath away. Eyes that had swept over his face and body with a quiet intensity, making him shiver and feel a hot hardening between his legs. Even later, he would experience that same heat when he thought of the man and wondered how it would feel to be locked in his arms, how he would taste and smell. Chris knew without a doubt that the man would haunt his dreams this night – and maybe many more nights.

Would he have the nerve to approach the guy if he showed up in the bar again? Probably not, he'd thought ruefully. The man was in a league of his own, and not likely to be enthralled with Chris' admiration, even from a distance.

His thoughts were abruptly interrupted as once more an elongated shadow was cast on the wall ahead of him. He cursed himself now for not accepting Randy, the maintenance guy's, offer to drive him home. But Randy was a moron – a moron who called him 'Blondie' and had bad breath and sticky palms...*ugh*. Chris had given the creep the brush off on more than one occasion, and getting in a car with him would have been tantamount to stupidity.

Just a hundred yards or so more and he'd be out on the main street and could hail a cab. Of course, he berated himself, if he'd used the brain he'd been born with, he would have called the cab and had it pick him up at the club door. With any luck, he'd have his own car back from the repair shop in a couple of days. For now, all he could do was keep walking and pray that whoever was tagging behind him was just some dude minding his own business and not someone who'd been lurking outside the gay club—someone intent on grabbing and beating the shit out of him in this long, dark alleyway.

Wait, if that was really his intention, wouldn't he have made his move by now?

Chris was almost at the end of the alley. He heard the sound of traffic and people's voices. His breathing calmed a little, and he found himself quickening his pace, almost running the last few yards that would take him out into the well-lit street where he would be surrounded by the late-night crowds thronging the sidewalks.

Only a few yards more, and he'd be safe.

Then *they* came out of the shadows in front of him. Three large, formidable figures that made Chris stop dead in his tracks. Fast as he could be on his feet, he knew there was no way around them in this narrow alley. They had spaced themselves across, forming a barrier of muscle and bone—and hatred.

"Hi, there…" The cold sneer in the voice brought up the short hairs on the back of Chris' neck. "What's a pretty little faggot like you doing out here so late?" The speaker, tall and bulky with thick shoulders, tapped the palm of one hand with the baseball bat he held in the other. "Lookin' to get a blow-job or somethin'?"

"I work at the Xtasy Club back there," Chris said, trying to keep the tremor of fear from his voice. "I'm just on my way home. I'm not looking for any trouble."

"Funny…" The guy with the baseball bat giggled, a sinister, unpleasant sound that made Chris' skin crawl. "'Cause trouble's lookin' for you." The other two men added quiet, insidious sniggers of their own at their friend's attempt at humour. "When we're done rearranging your pretty face, no one's gonna want a blow-job from you, *faggot*."

Chris' fingers, inside his pocket, flipped the top off the pepper-spray vial. They were going to hurt him without a doubt, but he'd go down with the satisfaction that at least one of them wouldn't be able to see for a while. He backed up a little, wondering if he could make it back to the safety of the club, where Joe the security guard could call the cops. No, he decided, he'd never make it. They'd be on him in a flash, beating the crap out of him with their fists, feet and that baseball bat. He shuddered as he imagined the pain these creeps were about to inflict on him.

On second thought, maybe running was definitely worth a try. He turned, ready to sprint as fast as he could towards the club, but before he'd gone more than three or four steps, he ran straight into a tall man's hard chest.

"Oof—" Chris staggered back until strong hands on his shoulders steadied him.

Four of them—oh *shit*. And this one was even taller than the others. Chris pulled the pepper spray from his pocket, ready to squirt the man's face. His hand was taken in a firm but gentle grip. His fingers were closed around the vial then he was lifted off his feet as if he weighed nothing at all and set down to one side. He peered up, trying to see the man's face, but the only nearby light shone behind the man's head and obscured Chris' vision.

"Gentlemen..." The man's slightly accented voice was soft and husky. "I suggest you put aside all thoughts of harming this young man and go about your business elsewhere."

All three thugs laughed raucously. "Oh, do you now?" The leader stepped forward, baseball bat raised, while the other two sidled up on either side of the tall man. "What if we take you, along with your faggot friend?"

"I would advise against trying that," the man said in that same calm, husky voice. "I will give you but one chance to leave here unhurt. Take this chance now or suffer the consequences."

"Fuck you!" The thug with the baseball bat lunged forward, bat raised to strike. The tall man's left hand shot out, gripping his assailant's wrist. Chris flinched as he heard the sound of snapping bone and a scream that was suddenly cut off. The thug slumped to the ground, laid out by a blow from the tall man's fist. The other two hesitated, stunned at seeing their friend put down so easily. Then, with an ugly snarl, one of them swung a punch at the man's head. With what looked to Chris like lightning speed, the man ducked and grabbed the second thug's fist in his own. Chris heard the sound of several bones breaking as the thug's arm was twisted into an extremely unnatural position. His scream too was cut short by a well-placed chop to the back of his neck.

The third, a skinny guy with a shock of carrot-red hair, obviously aware he had no chance against his taller opponent, made a dive for Chris — and into a stream of liquid pepper that burned his eyes and throat and sent him reeling back against the wall, gagging and trying to scream at the same time. Chris kicked him in the balls — hard. Choking and wheezing, the thug fell to his knees then keeled over, writhing in agony at Chris' feet.

"Thank you." Chris could barely get the words out. The adrenaline rush he'd experienced during the fight had evaporated, leaving him drained and shaken. He started to take a step towards the tall man, but instead he stumbled forward and would have fallen if the man had not caught him and pulled him into a strong embrace. For a moment, he was content to rest his face on the hard chest he was pressed to while he willed himself to stop shaking. He looked up at his protector, his face now illuminated by the light above them. Chris recognised him immediately — the strong features, the mane of black hair, those dark brooding eyes.

"You...you were in the bar earlier."

"Yes." The tall man gently brushed back the blond locks of hair that had spilled over Chris' forehead. "I saw you leave and wanted to make sure you would be safe. I...um...*anticipated* that you might have some trouble."

Chris stepped back a little and took the man's hand in his. "Uh...I'm Chris, by the way."

"I know." He smiled, showing white, even teeth. "I asked the bartender your name. I am Carlos Galeano."

"I'm very glad it was you following me." Chris smiled up at Carlos. "Although you gave me a nasty turn when I ran into you — literally." He looked down at the thugs who groaned with pain at their feet. "What do we do with these jerks?"

"You have a cell?"

"Yes."

"Call 9-1-1 and report a fight in this alley. We'll let the police take care of them while I take you for a glass of brandy. I'm sure you could use one right about now. You're still a little shaky."

"Thank you. Uh…I'll need my hand back to make the call."

"Of course." Carlos released Chris' hand with seeming reluctance. "My apologies."

"No, don't apologise." Chris smiled shyly. "It felt very nice."

* * * *

Later, as they walked together along Santa Monica Boulevard, Carlos asked, "Why do you work in that less than wholesome place?"

Chris chuckled. "You mean that dump? I need the money. In case you haven't noticed, LA is expensive. I'm studying for my MBA and I need to cover the rent and my car payment—so a little moonlighting on the side helps out. Lonnie, the owner, pays pretty well."

"I understand." He put his hand on Chris' arm as they approached a neon-lit sign that flashed the words, *Blue Moon*. "May I buy you a drink here?"

"That'd be great," Chris said, smiling up at the taller man. "But I should be buying after what you did for me back there."

They made their way into the noisy but warm and friendly atmosphere of the *Blue Moon*, and Chris waved to a couple of guys whose faces he recognised. One looked like he was about to come over to say hi, but then as he stared at Carlos, he seemed to change his mind and hung back, watching Chris and Carlos as they approached the bar.

"Is that a friend of yours?" Carlos asked.

"Not really—just a guy I kibitz with now and then when we run into one another."

"Would you like a brandy, or do you prefer something else?"

"Brandy's fine, thanks." Chris gazed with admiration at the man by his side as he ordered their drinks. *What a great looking guy*, he thought, *and he seems so nice*. He shuddered as he thought back to that moment in the alley when he'd been confronted by those redneck jerks. He'd most likely be a pile of broken and bloody flesh lying in the dark if Carlos hadn't intervened. As the tall man turned to hand Chris his drink, Chris noticed for the first time that the eyes that gazed at him with such warmth were a dark brown, flecked with gold, and framed by long thick lashes. When Carlos smiled, he had a dimple on each cheek, and he was younger than Chris had first thought, his face smooth and unlined. Chris found he couldn't resist reaching up to kiss his defender on the lips.

"Thank you," Chris murmured. "Thanks for saving my life tonight."

Carlos smiled into the Chris' eyes. "It is not your destiny to die at the hands of cowardly thugs," he said huskily. "Fate has set aside a life of love and adventure for you."

Chris resisted the temptation to laugh. What Carlos had just said sounded like it belonged in a fortune cookie—except Carlos seemed dead serious.

"You can see into the future?"

"No." Carlos handed Chris his drink. "*Salud*." He clinked Chris' glass with his. "But sometimes I can tell if a person's life is to be lively or humdrum."

"Well, I certainly like the idea of love and adventure." Chris smiled at Carlos. "I've never been in love, and the most adventurous thing I've ever done was get on the Ride of Death at Magic Mountain."

Carlos chuckled. "I understand that particular ride is on the scary side."

"Scared the crap outta me," Chris said then took a long swig of his drink. "So, what on earth were you doing in a dump like the Xtasy Club? I wouldn't think a dive like that is your style at all."

"It's not, but I saw you go in and followed you."

"Oh, really?" Chris felt himself blush at the obvious inference.

"Yes. I didn't realise you actually worked there until I saw you enter the office. I had imagined you were merely going in for a drink, and I thought I might engage you in conversation, buy you a drink — that kind of thing."

Chris grinned up at him. "Engage me in conversation? You're not from around here, are you?"

"No, I am Spanish — from Madrid."

"You're on vacation?"

"Yes. I'm staying with friends in the hills of Hollywood."

Chris chuckled. "It's Hollywood Hills, but I like it better the way you say it."

"May I ask what Chris is short for?" Carlos asked. "Christian or Christopher?"

"Christopher." Chris smiled. "But only my mother calls me that."

"It is a beautiful name—Christopher." Carlos pronounced it by accenting the first syllable.

"Again, I like the way *you* say it," Chris said, his smile widening. "It must be that sexy accent."

"Then you won't mind if I call you Christopher?"

"Not at all."

"And what does your mother think of you working in that less-than-stellar establishment?" Carlos asked with a teasing tone.

Chris grimaced. "She'd have a fit if she knew—so I haven't told her or my dad. They'd offer to help out with the rent, and I really want to be independent. They live in Santa Barbara, so they don't need to know everything I do. Besides," he added almost defensively, "I'm not a kid. I've been living on my own for two years. I can take care of myself." He sighed ruefully. "At least, I thought I could until tonight."

Carlos smiled and gently squeezed Chris' shoulder. "Well, you couldn't be expected to take on three mindless bullies at once. I'm sure that under normal circumstances you could take care of yourself very well."

"Tell my folks that—they hate the fact I live in LA. They're convinced this city's full of degenerates." Chris laughed lightly. "I mean, there are some of those around, but there're some really cool people here, too."

Carlos eyed two empty stools at a nearby table.

"Would you care to sit for a while?"

Carlos was anxious to find out more about this charmingly unaffected young man. Innately, he knew that it was not just by accident that he had seen him earlier entering the Xtasy Club. Fate, destiny, rather than mere chance had guided his footsteps towards a place he would not normally have dreamed of entering. He could have assumed that perhaps fate had simply wanted him to be there to save the young man from a vicious beating, but no, there was more to it than that. He could already feel the beginning of a bond between them, stronger even than that of protector, although Carlos knew that he would go to any lengths to protect Christopher.

Chapter Two

As they settled themselves at the table, Chris looked up at Carlos with a shy smile, drinking in the man's strong features, getting ready to pinch himself.

"What?" Carlos asked gently.

"I'm beginning to feel as though this is some kind of dream," Chris said, his eyes meeting Carlos' steady gaze. "I mean, a few minutes ago you were saving me from being beaten up by a bunch of jerks. I really felt at that moment I'd had it then there you were like some avenging angel beating the crap out of them—and now here I am, having a quiet drink with the handsome stranger who came along in the nick o' time. Not many people could claim to have had this happen to them. I bet most people who get mugged in the street get stepped on or totally ignored."

Carlos chuckled. "Let's just say I was in the right place at the right time."

"Yeah, but you took on all three at once. Where did you learn to fight like that?"

"Uh, while I was at the university in Madrid, I took some self-defence classes. But I only took care of two of them. You managed the third coward all by yourself."

"Well, only because you were there." He touched Carlos' hand gently. "Thanks again."

Carlos took Chris' hand in his and raised it to his lips. He lingered over the warm skin, inhaling the fresh scent. His eyes met Chris', and for a moment, both men remained very still while the atmosphere between them crackled with intensity.

"You are a very beautiful young man," Carlos murmured, still holding Chris' hand near his lips.

"Th-thanks," Chris stuttered. "And you are...you are *more* than that." He blushed. "I just don't have the words to describe you. I've never met anyone quite like you in my life. I still think this is some kind of dream."

Carlos' smile deepened the dimples on his cheeks. "A pleasant one, I hope."

"Pleasant is hardly the word — fantastic is more like it."

"This is *fantastic* for me also."

"Would you like to get out of here?" Chris faltered for a moment, praying that Carlos wouldn't think him too pushy. "I...uh, my place is quite near, just a ten minute walk from here."

Carlos kissed Chris' hand and winked at him. "But only five, if we run."

"Like the wind," Chris whispered. "Let's go."

* * * *

They didn't exactly run, but there was definitely some brisk walking involved, and Chris was a bit breathless by the time they'd hurried up the steps to his apartment. He was glad he'd tidied the place up before he'd left for work. He didn't want Carlos to think he was a slob.

"Come on in," he said, unlocking the apartment door. "It's not much, but I call it home."

"Thank you for inviting me into your home," Carlos said, looking around at the tasteful furnishings. "It's charming."

"Let me take your coat. Aren't you a little warm with that on?"

"Not really." Carlos slipped his coat from his shoulders. "I'm a little cold-blooded at the best of times. California is sunny, but I find the nights quite cool."

"Madrid is warmer?" Chris asked, laying the coat over an armchair.

"At night, yes," Carlos replied.

His eyes met Chris' and held them locked to his. Chris shivered with anticipation as he moved into Carlos' arms, tilting his head back to meet the kiss he longed for. Their lips met and meshed, soft moist flesh bonding, binding them together in a moment of complete rapture. The tip of Chris' tongue moved across Carlos' lower lip seeking entrance, and as the other man's mouth opened to give him access, he felt as if he were melting into Carlos' very being. So intensely erotic was the sensation that all he wanted to see, feel and smell was the man who now held him, caressed him and stole his breath in that long searing kiss.

Carlos' tongue was everywhere inside Chris' mouth, probing, teasing, bringing him a tumult of sensation that caused him to moan and move even deeper into the bigger man's embrace. Hands that tugged at his shirt and peeled it from his body stroked and caressed his torso, lips moved over his jaw, his throat, leaving a searing sensuous trail of fire on his skin. Chris, even in his limited experience, knew instinctively that what was happening between Carlos and himself was extraordinary. He had never been made love to like this in his entire life. He had never anticipated that anyone could bring him the kind of passion or desire that this man created within him. It was almost too much, almost unbearable. He wanted to shout with joy, but all that escaped his lips was a whimper, a plea to be taken, to be consumed, to be *owned* by Carlos.

He felt himself being lifted into Carlos' arms without any seeming effort. He wrapped his legs around Carlos' narrow waist while Carlos buried his face in Chris' chest, licking and nibbling at his nipples. Chris suddenly realised they were both naked—when had that happened?

But who cares? Chris thought, revelling in the pleasure of Carlos' bare flesh pressed to his. He wound his arms about Carlos' neck and found his mouth again in another long and rapturous kiss. Then they were in his bedroom, and Chris wasn't quite sure how that had happened either, but again his senses were blurred by the sensations of the kiss he never wanted to end.

Carlos lowered him onto the bed and lay over him. Chris felt the heat and pulse of the man's erection as it slid over his own eagerly throbbing cock. The pre-cum that spilled from both their cocks mingled on Chris' stomach, and Carlos lowered his head to lick at it before taking Chris' hard shaft into his mouth, bearing down on it all the way to the base. Chris gasped as yet another new sensation swept over him, the sure knowledge that Carlos too was completely caught up in the rapture they were sharing. Sensation and emotion mixed with his feelings of sheer physical elation at being made love to by this incredible man.

Chris didn't know how he could be so sure of what Carlos was feeling—he just knew. It was as though Carlos had somehow touched his mind, to let him know that this was much more than merely physical— that their minds as well as their bodies were as one. Chris felt a slow tingling in his spine as that thought enveloped him. Never had he experienced a feeling as *intimate* as this. With a moan of total surrender, he gave himself up to the exquisite pleasure Carlos brought him as his lips and tongue worked their own brand of magic on Chris' hard, pulsing flesh. He wanted to do the same for Carlos, if he could. He found himself wishing he was more experienced, that he had more expertise in bringing pleasure to another man. The total number of times he'd actually gone this far with any one man he could count on his left hand—and truth to tell, he'd never felt this undeniable need before.

Carlos gently released Chris' cock from his mouth and leant over him, kissing his lips tenderly. His eyes met Chris', and he smiled as he murmured, "You are bringing me more pleasure than you can ever know. Just lie there and let me love you."

Chris gazed up into the dark, golden brown eyes locked on his. He reached up to stroke Carlos' smooth jaw then let his hand glide over a wide shoulder, down across Carlos' hard, sculpted chest. "I want you to feel as good as I do," he whispered. "I've never met anyone like you—never experienced anything like this."

Carlos' smile deepened. "And I have never met anyone quite as adorable as you."

"Really? A man like you…?"

"I am just a man, Christopher, a man who considers himself fortunate to be able to hold someone as beautiful as you in my arms and make love to you over and over."

Startled, yet deeply touched by what Carlos had just said, Chris found himself unable to form a reply, but his parted lips invoked an invitation Carlos did not refuse. His mouth closed over Chris' in a kiss that was still tender but with a hungry demanding edge that had both men moaning with need and desire. Carlos' hand slid down the length of Chris' spine then cupped the round swell of his butt, pulling him in closer. The sensation of having this strong, hard body pressed to his overwhelmed Chris' senses, filling him with a carnal longing to be possessed completely, to have Carlos take him body and soul. He almost cried out as the need overtook him, and as if Carlos had read his mind, his fingers slipped between Chris' butt cheeks, probing at the tight ring of muscle, easing into the soft, silken heat beyond his resistance.

Chris' body bucked from the sensation that swept through his blood. He arched his back, pushing his ass against Carlos' fingers, drawing him deeper inside himself, shuddering with ecstasy as his sweet spot was probed and caressed. He whimpered with longing, pressing himself even further into Carlos' embrace as if melting into his flesh and becoming one with him was the only thing that would bring him total satisfaction.

"Fuck me, please." Chris' face grew hot as he whispered the words. He'd never asked it of anyone before, and now, here he was almost begging this man to take him in a manner he'd never really enjoyed. It was just that he was so sure, with Carlos, it would be everything he'd always hoped for.

Carlos withdrew his fingers and turned Chris over onto his stomach. Sitting astride Chris' thighs, he stroked and massaged the smooth and lightly tanned flesh beneath him then leant forward to kiss the nape of Chris' neck. His lips wove an erotic pattern down the length of Chris' spine, coming to rest at the cleft between his buttocks where he laid a kiss on either cheek before parting them to allow his tongue access to Chris' moist hole. Chris moaned aloud as Carlos laved the ring of tight muscle surrounding his opening. His body writhed, his hands clutched at the sheets beneath him as the tip of Carlos' tongue entered him, bringing him to such an exquisite ecstasy, he thought for a moment he might lose all control and come too soon. He wanted all of Carlos inside him before that happened. He had just about enough reason left to reach for the nightstand drawer. Pulling it open, he slipped a condom packet into the palm of his hand and passed it back to Carlos then reached for the lube — lots of lube.

Carlos took the tube and coated his fingers, slipping one then two deep inside Chris' ass. His fingers moved inside Chris, stretching his tight hole and, once more, bringing him to the brink of delirious joy. Chris raised his hips slightly as he felt the head of Carlos' cock nudge at his opening. He held his breath, willing himself not to wince or cry out with the pain he was sure would accompany Carlos entering him. The tight ring of muscle protecting his opening gave up its resistance under the pressure of the hard, rigid flesh that pushed into him — then, not pain, at least not the excruciating pain he'd experienced once before, just an exquisite sharp burn that had him arching his back in surprise, followed by a feeling of intense exhilaration as Carlos pressed forward, driving every sensational, hard inch of his cock all the way inside him.

"Oh, yes!"

His cry of deep satisfaction was echoed by Carlos as he plunged in and out of Chris, his rhythm matched by the adorable man who writhed under him, bringing him a fulfilment he had not known for so long.

Yes, this was what he had craved for, hungered for all these empty years, someone who not only gave him his body, but his mind and soul. Combined with the raw physical need expressed in both their longings was a tenderness, an emotion that went beyond the carnal, emotion that Carlos had not experienced in a long time. He pulled himself to his knees, lifting Chris so that his back was pressed to Carlos' chest. Carlos wrapped his arms tightly around Chris' body, holding him in an embrace neither man wanted to end. He raised his hips upward to meet Chris' downward push, his cock sinking even deeper inside Chris. Chris' head fell back onto Carlos' wide shoulder, his blissful moans muffled by Carlos' lips covering his mouth with a lingering and sensuous kiss.

His lips moved to Chris' neck where the scent of the sweet blood coursing through Chris' jugular made his mind reel with need. His fangs lengthened, nipping gently at the smooth skin. Calling on all his willpower, he turned his head away, denying himself the life-giving human elixir.

Not yet, not yet. Not until he is willing.

Locking Chris to him with one arm, Carlos let his free hand glide down over Chris' torso, reaching for the hot, throbbing flesh that jutted so proudly from between Chris' thighs.

"Yes, my love," he murmured, his lips pressed to Chris' ear. "Come for me." The lithe young man shuddered in his embrace. Cries of sheer pleasure were wrung from Chris as his body arched in total rapture and his orgasm was ripped from him, sending a torrent of semen arcing across the bed sheets. Carlos held him even tighter, laving his neck and throat with wet urgent kisses. His hips bucked faster now, driving his hard-as-steel cock into Chris' hot core until he could hold back no longer, and he exploded into the condom with great, gut-wrenching spasms.

Chris curved an arm round Carlos' neck, turning his head, seeking a kiss from the man who had brought him to a plane of ecstasy he had never until this moment known existed. Still trembling with emotion, he was content to stay secure in Carlos' embrace and to feel the pulsing of the man's cock, still buried deep inside him.

"I think I've just been to heaven and back," he whispered against the soft lips that caressed his.

"And you took me with you." Carlos eased them both into a side-by-side position without pulling free of him. Chris clenched down on the still-hard flesh that filled him and pushed himself deeper into Carlos' arms.

Chris took one of the big hands that held him fast and raised it to his lips. "Will you stay with me tonight?"

"I wish I could." Carlos nuzzled Chris' ear. "But I have an extremely early morning appointment."

Chris shifted slightly so that he could see Carlos' face. "I thought you were on vacation."

Carlos smiled. "Business mixed with pleasure."

"But I'll see you again?"

"You will—that you can depend on."

"Then, that's okay." Chris lifted his head to kiss Carlos on his soft, full lips. "But you don't have to leave just yet, do you?"

Carlos smiled down at him. "No, I do not."

"Mmm…" Chris clenched his ass muscles around Carlos' hardening cock. "You feel as though you're ready to go again."

"Ready when you are."

"Oh, I'm ready." Chris wrapped his arms about Carlos' neck and pulled him down for another long kiss. "Let's go."

Chapter Three

Carlos let himself into the big house his friends owned in the Hollywood Hills. He entered the impressive reception hall and stood for moment, listening to the sounds of a violin being played in the drawing room.

Tony... What an incredible talent, he thought. Silently, so as not to disturb the musician or his audience of three, he moved across the tiled floor and waited in the drawing room doorway until the last strains of the melody had died away. It gave him a moment or two to look, with some fondness, upon the beautiful form and face of his cousin, the Lady Andorra, as she gave her lover, Tony, her rapt attention. His gaze shifted to the man who sat by his cousin's side — his lifelong friend Marcus Verano, truly the handsomest man he had ever known. Carlos retained a special affection for Marcus, for it was he who had comforted Andorra in her time of grief for the family she had lost to the vile actions of the Comte d'Arcy.

The attractive young man who sat nestled close to Marcus, Carlos had known only recently but had already formed a warm friendship with, was Roger Folsom — a mortal when he and Marcus had first met and fallen in love, but who had been changed through, once again, the evil machinations of their enemy, the Comte d'Arcy. A pity, Carlos had reflected many a time, that Marcus had sent d'Arcy into hiding. He would loved to have torn the contemptible Comte to shreds.

"Bravo, Tony!"

Carlos smiled as Marcus jumped to his feet, applauding with enthusiasm.

He turned to smile at Carlos. "Carlos, you have just missed hearing Tony's new composition."

"I heard the last few bars, and it sounded beautiful, Tony."

"Thanks." Tony's mop of unruly, dark-brown hair had fallen across his forehead, hiding his thick brows, but his eyes twinkled with pleasure. He turned to accept a kiss on his cheek from the beautiful woman who slipped a proprietary arm around his waist.

"My Tony is a genius," Andorra purred, hugging her man to her side.

"Indeed he is," Carlos agreed. He bent slightly and leant in to kiss Andorra lightly on both cheeks. "You look beautiful as ever, my dear cousin."

Andorra smiled and tapped Carlos gently on his chin with her forefinger. "And where were you when Tony and I arrived? Marcus and Roger were expecting you earlier."

"My apologies." Carlos smiled at his hosts. "I was detained by a most interesting and delightful young mortal."

"Ah..." Marcus grinned at him. "I thought it must have been something quite pressing."

"Pressing the flesh you mean," Roger said, winking at Carlos. "Anyone I know?"

"We didn't get as far as exchanging our friends' names," Carlos replied, chuckling. "His name is Chris Jeffries, although I asked if I may call him Christopher. He is studying to be an accountant and has a part time job at the Xtasy Club, off Santa Monica."

Roger grimaced. "Ugh, that dump."

"It's not the best of places," Carlos agreed. "Nor the safest," he added after a pause.

"You had trouble?" Marcus asked.

"Some thugs were out to beat Chris...Christopher to a pulp, so I stepped in and stopped them."

"And now, he's yours forever," Roger sighed. "You're his hero."

"Actually, he defended himself very well," Carlos said with a trace of admiration in his voice. "He showed he could be calm and courageous when faced with armed cowards."

"How romantic," Andorra remarked dryly, shaking her head. "You and your one-night love affairs, Carlos. It is time you found a forever companion again."

"Would you care for some wine?" Marcus asked quickly.

"I'll get it," Tony said as Carlos nodded after a sharp look at Andorra. "I think I could use a martini right about now."

"No, I mean it," Andorra insisted. "You have been alone too long, Carlos."

"*Andy*," Tony said in a warning tone as he poured a dark red wine into a crystal glass. "Carlos doesn't want to talk about it."

"But I do," Andorra said, ignoring Tony's warning. "We have all lost loved ones. Marcus and I can attest to that."

"Andorra," Marcus murmured. "Now is not the time."

Carlos gave him a tight smile as he accepted the wine from Tony. "It's all right, Marcus. My dear cousin delights in meddling in my affairs."

"I do not meddle, Carlos," Andorra sniffed. "I merely want you to be happy."

"I am happy." Carlos' smile widened. "In fact, tonight I have never been happier."

"He was that good, eh?" Roger teased, his blue eyes glinting.

They shared a smile. "He was—*is*—a very interesting young man," Carlos said.

"So you're seeing him again?"

"I'm planning on it."

"Great!" Roger positively beamed. "When do we get to meet him?"

"Uh…that may take some time to arrange."

"Why? Hey, Marcus laid it all out for me the first night we were together."

Carlos chuckled. "We are not all as self-assured as Marcus."

"Oh, come now, Carlos," Marcus said with a light laugh. "I have never known you to be unsure of your considerable charm."

"Well, let's just say I want to *very* sure before I reveal my true nature to him."

"You didn't take a little sip?" Roger asked with an impish smile.

"No, I did not." Carlos grimaced for a moment. "That is not to say I wasn't tempted. I was. But I felt something more than just a hunger for his blood. The waiting will be hard, of course."

Andorra sighed impatiently. "Why bother? You will have discarded him and made him forget you as you have done with so many others over the years. Ever since Miguel died, you have—"

"Andorra!" Carlos glared at his cousin through narrowed eyes. "I have asked you repeatedly not to mention Miguel's name. If you cannot honour my request, perhaps it is time I made *you* forget!"

"*Carlos*." Andorra stared back at him, her beautiful face shadowed by shock.

Tony moved away from the bar and came to stand by her. "Carlos," he said quietly putting a defensive arm around her. "Andy didn't mean anything by it."

Carlos' glare swept away from his cousin and fixed on Tony's frowning expression. He let out a long, hissing breath from between his teeth, but his shoulders visibly relaxed as his gaze softened. He bowed his head slightly.

"My apologies, Andorra...Tony. I'm afraid the memory of that time is still like an open wound on my soul."

"Oh, Carlos..." Andorra stepped forward and embraced him. "I am sorry. Sometimes my tongue is faster than my brain. I know how much you loved him—how much we all loved him."

"I apologise again, Andorra. But for your quick actions all those years ago, I would not be here today. And you're right. It's time I put the past to rest and looked to the future."

Roger had been transfixed by the scene played out in front of him. Now, he saw a chance to lighten the atmosphere. "And this Chris guy might just be the one to help you with that," he said.

"Well, it's a little early."

"Nah. I knew soon as I looked at the big guy here," Roger continued, beaming up at Marcus. "And Ron knew the first time he clapped eyes on Jean-Claude. And Micah—"

"All right, Roger," Marcus said, chuckling. "I think we get the picture. You're a great believer in love at first sight."

The friends smiled as the moment of tension passed, but later, alone in his room, his cousin Andorra's words rankled in Carlos' mind. Was it so obvious to them all that the past years of his existence had been spent searching for what he could never find—a devotion as deep and as rich as the love he'd shared with Miguel?

So many times, in his loneliness, he had considered himself fortunate in having family and friends he could turn to for solace and companionship. Most of all, Andorra, his cousin, to whom he had run on the night he had been savaged by vampires, knowing only she could help him. If he had listened to her warnings, of course, there would have been no need for her protection. If he had not ventured into the den of darkness, lured by the handsome lord whose reputation was anything but pure. If he had resisted the carnal desire with which the man infused him, then all that had transpired would have been... Been what? Nothing... *Nothing*.

Carlos groaned as these dark memories flooded his mind. He had ignored his cousin Andorra's warning, even though he knew of the dark realm from which she too had tried to escape those years ago. He and Andorra had been the only survivors — the rest of her family taken in a hideous and terror-stricken manner. For years he had tried to put these terrible memories to rest. Why now were they foremost in his mind? Why, after the most wondrous evening he had spent in as long as he could remember?

But some memories linger, and he would never forget his and Andorra's flight to France to try to stop the Comte d'Arcy from making good his promise to kill all of Andorra's family if she and her younger brother Anton did not give themselves up for his pleasure. They had arrived too late. Anton had committed suicide rather than be a vampire's plaything, and the Comte had taken a terrible revenge, killing Andorra's parents and sisters in a brutal and callous fashion. How Carlos had missed her during the years of her seclusion when she had shut herself away from the world to mourn the loss of her family and to never forgive the monster who had taken them from her.

Wrenching himself from the memories his cousin's words had brought him, he brought before him the sweet vision of the young man he had made love to so few hours ago.

"Christopher," he whispered. "Can you be the one who will heal my soul? I did not erase the memory of our time together as I have done with so many others in the past. I have a deep and desirous wish to see you again. To hold you again. To love you again." Carlos sighed as he brought the image of Chris' face into sharp focus. The fine bones, the tousled fair hair, the large light-blue eyes that had so quickly darkened with lust during their lovemaking, the soft, full mouth...

He'd had sex with many mortals over the years, but few had touched him as Christopher had. Just as Andorra had pointed out, it was his habit to make those young men forget him, often after their first meeting, and as Andorra had also stated on more than one occasion, even though she knew it angered him, he did it only because none, not one, could ever compare with Miguel.

Of course, she was right.

Miguel had not only been a beautiful man in appearance, his soul had held a radiance that shone through his eyes, captivating all who ever met him and those who grew to know him well. Andorra had introduced them a few short years after Carlos had been changed. Carlos could still remember that night when she had brought the tall, darkly blond Navarran before him.

"Carlos," she had said in that sultry voice that had captured a hundred men's hearts when she was a mortal woman, "I would like you to meet Miguel Ramirez. Miguel,

this is my cousin, Carlos Galeano." She had left them almost immediately, drifting across the room, a vision of elegance and beauty in a crystal-beaded, silk gown of deepest burgundy.

Miguel had smiled into Carlos' eyes, and Carlos was lost in that smile, the attraction he felt for the other man bringing him the start of an arousal that made his pale skin flush slightly with discomfort.

"Your cousin is a most beautiful woman," Miguel said, touching Carlos' arm, indicating that they should walk outside into the cool night air.

"Yes, she is."

"And it seems to be a family trait," he continued, his eyes sweeping over Carlos' face and body.

Carlos laughed lightly. "Thank you, but few can compare to the Lady Andorra."

"Few women, perhaps..." Miguel's eyes, a radiant blue, locked on Carlos as he spoke, his voice low and husky and incredibly beguiling.

Carlos did not miss the invitation in those eyes, nor did he refuse it. With one swift movement, he drew Miguel into his arms, holding him in a tight embrace, their lips meeting in a bruising and passionate kiss. As their tongues meshed and caressed, Carlos probed the razor-like sharpness of Miguel's fangs. His blood spilled onto Miguel's tongue from the self-inflicted cut, and the rich taste of it inflamed the senses of both men.

Miguel's arms tightened about Carlos. "Come away with me," he urged. "Come to my house, and let me love you until the dawn's light."

Carlos sighed as those memories of their first night together came back to haunt him, again. One hundred years had passed since Miguel's death, a short span of time in a vampire's existence, and through all that time, he had never forgotten him, nor found someone to love as he had loved Miguel. Sometimes, he could understand Andorra's impatience, even if her voicing it irritated him.

Perhaps she was right. He had been alone too long. Perhaps it was time to explore new possibilities. Around the edges of the thick window shutters, Carlos saw the faint traces of approaching dawn. He stripped off his clothes and slipped between the cool sheets. When he closed his eyes, a vision of Christopher's sweet face swam before him, and he smiled. Not in as long as he could remember had he ever sought to retain the memory of those with whom he'd had sex. They remembered only what he allowed of the encounter, and he would so quickly and easily forget them—but not this time, not Christopher. For in Carlos' mind, what he and Christopher had shared, had not been mere sex, it had been much, much more and had touched his soul.

Chapter Four

Chris sat staring at his computer screen, trying to concentrate on the words and figures before his eyes. He had an exam at the end of the week, and the online crash course he'd signed up for wasn't doing it for him. For three days and nights, he had thought of nothing and no one but Carlos, the fantastic man who had saved him from a vicious beating, who had made love to him like only some fantasy lover could—and who had then vanished without a trace. Chris had fallen asleep in shelter of the man's arms and when he'd awoken, Carlos had been gone. He'd looked for him in the club, hoping that he would see that tall, familiar figure standing at the bar, his dark mysterious eyes searching the crowd, searching for no one but—

"Me!" Chris blurted, pushing his chair away from the computer desk and jumping to his feet. He paced his small living room, a desperate, frustrated mood clouding his mind. Why hadn't he come back? Had their night together meant so little to him? He'd been so loving, so completely into what they'd shared. Chris had been sure of that at the time—but now?

Am I so naïve that I have to suppose it meant as much to him as it did to me? he thought, shaking his head sadly. *A man like that, so beautiful and sophisticated, must have his pick of anyone he wants—and what do I have to offer him? Only myself…and obviously that isn't enough.*

Sighing, he sat down again at his desk and resumed staring at the screen in front of him, trying again to concentrate on the test. A little chime told him he had mail. Carlos? *Don't be silly*, he chided himself. Carlos hadn't asked for his email address—or his phone number, now he came to think about it. He really hadn't wanted to keep in touch.

The email was from his friend Joey.

Wanna go 4 a beer? meet u at the blue moon in 20.

He emailed back.

Sure—c u there.

Might as well. Joey was always good company. They'd been friends since junior high—two gay boys protecting each other from the bullies who had lurked in the locker rooms and shadowy corridors. The so-called jocks had always been ready to pounce on and beat the shit out of any 'fag' who strayed their way. The guys who had tried to beat him up in the alley were most likely products of that same environment. But Joey and he had formed a close bond that had grown stronger with the years, and Chris had become the rock Joey turned to when his heart was broken—which, Chris reflected with a rueful grin, was just about three times a year. Joey hated being without a boyfriend, and his eagerness to see only the good qualities in them often left him crushed by their flakiness. Fortunately, after the last disaster, Joey didn't seem in any hurry to make another mistake.

Chris took a moment to brush his teeth and run a comb through his hair then picked up his bomber jacket. He was headed for the door when a gentle knock stopped him in his tracks.

Who…?

He flung open the door then gasped with surprise and no small measure of delight at the sight of the tall, dark-haired man who stood framed in the doorway, smiling down at him.

"Carlos," he whispered. "Come in."

Carlos' smile deepened, and he stepped inside. He glanced at the bomber jacket Chris held. "You were going out?"

Chris threw the jacket onto a chair. "No…well, yeah, but I can cancel. Joey'll understand. I'll call him right now."

"I don't want to spoil your plans."

"No, you won't," Chris assured him. "I was just meeting my friend Joey for a beer. He won't mind, and I'd rather spend time with you," he added shyly.

"Thank you." Carlos smiled into Chris' eyes then leant in to kiss his lips gently. "It's good to see you again."

"Yes, it is—I mean, it's good to see *you* again." The kiss had left him slightly breathless. "Let me just call Joey… Take off your coat. Make yourself at home."

"I brought some wine for us to share."

"Great." He punched in Joey's number while Carlos removed his leather coat and hung it over the back of a chair. "Joey? Hey, I'm sorry. Can I catch you later? I forgot I had a friend coming round."

"Anyone I know?"

"Not yet, but you'll get to meet him."

"*All right.* Okay, I'll call you tomorrow. Have fun tonight."

"Talk at you later. Bye, Joey."

He grinned at Carlos. "Just a little white lie. Gee, it's good to see you." He paused for a moment then decided to throw caution to the wind. "I was beginning to think you didn't want to see me again. I hoped you'd come to the club. We didn't exchange any numbers or anything, so there was no way I could reach you."

"I apologise. My friends had invited my cousin and her, uh, *fiancée* for a short visit. They left an hour ago, and I came straight here after bidding them goodbye. I hope you don't mind my not calling in advance."

"No, not all," Chris said quickly, slightly in awe of Carlos' formal manners. *Was everyone in Spain this polite?*

Carlos held out a hand to him, and Chris let himself be drawn into the taller man's embrace. He sighed with happiness as he pressed his lips to the cool skin of Carlos' neck, shivering with anticipation as the man's mouth took his in a kiss that was both sweet and passionate.

When finally Carlos pulled back slightly, he murmured, "Since we were together, I have thought of little else but when I would see you again. I'm sorry I did not call on you sooner."

Chris felt a surge of happiness at those words. He tilted his head back to receive another kiss, his arms encircling Carlos' narrow waist, holding him tightly pressed to his own body. Once again, Chris felt like he was dreaming. He'd hoped for this, wished for it—and now, it had happened. Carlos was here holding him against his thrilling body, kissing him breathless, making him weak at the knees—and hot damn, but it felt so good! Everything about this man had him enthralled. Not just his beautiful face and body. It was more than that. It was his warmth and sincerity, and the way he made Chris feel needed—*wanted.*

"I'm so glad you're here," he murmured breathlessly, in between kisses.

"I would like to ask you something," Carlos said quietly.

"Anything..."

"Can we sit awhile? Perhaps drink a glass of wine?"

"Sure." Chris smiled at him happily. "I'll get us a couple of glasses." He ran behind the bar that separated the tiny kitchen from the living room and carefully brought two crystal glasses from one of the cabinets.

Carlos eyed the glasses with faint surprise as Chris put them on the bar top. "They are very beautiful," he said, sliding onto a bar stool.

"My grandmother's." Chris sighed sadly. "She passed a year ago and left me these, and some other stuff that I keep at my parents' house."

Carlos picked up the glass by its delicate stem. "Very old, too."

"Yeah, antique. I think they were *her* grandmother's. I only use them for special occasions — like tonight." He smiled at Carlos and handed him a corkscrew. "*Very* special occasions…"

Carlos returned his smile. "Thank you." He opened the wine bottle and poured a small amount into one of the glasses. He passed the glass to Chris. "Try a little, savour it." He watched as Chris inhaled the bouquet then took a tiny sip, letting the wine rest on his tongue before swallowing it slowly. Carlos gazed at him, enthralled by the sight of the muscles in Chris' throat moving sensually under his skin. He felt his cock lengthen and harden. His need to taste Chris' sweet blood, to possess him, was so powerful it almost overwhelmed him.

With a supreme effort, he calmed himself and said, his voice low and husky, "You know how to appreciate a fine wine."

Chris grinned. "My folks own a vineyard in Santa Barbara. I was brought up appreciating good wine — and this is very nice. French I'd say, not Californian."

"I'm impressed. *Chateau-Neuf-du-Pape*, a good vintage." He poured them both a glass. "So, if your parents are successful, why did you leave home?"

"The idea is, once I get my MBA, I'll handle the business accounts for them. I could have done all this in Santa Barbara, but I just wanted to get way for a while — you know, experience life a little before I settle into the business."

"And have you experienced life a little?"

"Not until I met you." Chris blushed slightly. "I…I mean, you've made me more aware of…of what I want from my life."

Carlos raised his glass and brought it gently to Chris'. "And you have touched my life in much the same way, Christopher. *Salud*."

"*Salud*, Carlos. I am very glad we met."

"As am I…" They drank, Chris' eyes meeting Carlos' sultry gaze over the rims of their glasses.

"You said you wanted to ask me something," Chris ventured.

Carlos nodded, patting the barstool beside him. He waited until Chris came from behind the bar and climbed onto the stool next to him.

"I have a business proposition for you."

"Business?"

"Yes. I need someone to handle my financial accounts here in the States. As you will soon be an accountant, I'd like to offer you the position."

"But I haven't even passed my exams yet."

"But you will at the end of the week."

"How did you know that? That I have exams, I mean?'"

"I believe you mentioned it on our first night together."

"I did?" Chris frowned for a moment. "I can't believe I mentioned something as boring as that in the middle of what we were doing." He blushed again. "I mean…well, you know what I mean."

Carlos chuckled and leant forward to kiss Chris' lips. "Yes, I know what you mean. So, will you accept the position?"

"I'd love to. What is your business, exactly?"

"I buy and sell antiques," Carlos replied. "It means I have to travel, sometimes to quite out of the way places. I would expect you to accompany me on occasion."

"Wow, that sounds terrific. Now, I really will have to pass these exams."

"You will do very well, Christopher. I know it."

"Thanks for the vote of confidence. I'm a little nervous."

Carlos stood and put his arms around Chris. "There is no need for you to be nervous. His lips touched Chris' neck. "And now, we will put business aside and enjoy our wine—and each other."

"I'm all for that," Chris murmured, shivering as Carlos' lips skimmed over his throat. He fell forward into the taller man's embrace. "Oh, but that feels so good..." He slipped off the stool and pressed himself against the hard wall of muscle that was Carlos' chest. "All of you feels so good." He started to undo Carlos' shirt buttons. "Want to kiss that perfect chest of yours. I remember it being smooth. Yes, there it is—smooth and perfect."

Carlos rumbled out a deep chuckle and enfolded Chris in his arms. "Have I told you, you are adorable?"

"I think you mentioned it a few times," Chris said, in between the kisses he laid on Carlos' chest. "Took me a time to believe you weren't just saying it to get into my pants."

"But I did get into your pants."

"Yeah..." Chris' eyes twinkled as he smiled up at Carlos. "Guess I'm just that easy." He took Carlos' hand and led him into the bedroom. "And guess what? You're going to get into my pants again. Right now."

Carlos cupped Chris' face in his hands and kissed his lips tenderly. Chris let out a little moan and parted his lips, letting their kiss deepen and Carlos' tongue slip inside his mouth. He pulled Carlos' unbuttoned shirt over his shoulders, eager to feel the strong cool flesh, to caress the smooth skin that covered Carlos' muscular back. His hands skimmed down the length of Carlos' spine then pushed their way under the waistband of Carlos' slacks, cupping each cheek of his muscular butt. He shivered with anticipation, feeling the rigidity of Carlos' arousal grind into his groin.

He slipped from the tall man's arms and knelt before him, unbuckling the leather belt and easing his slacks down over his hips. He murmured his admiration at the powerful sight of Carlos' erection as it sprang from its confinement. Grasping the thick shaft at its base, Chris brought the swollen head to his lips, his tongue snaking out to lick the glistening slit at the tip. The pungent spicy taste and scent of Carlos' pre-cum assaulted his senses, bringing a tumult of desire coursing through his body. Without hesitating, he took all of the throbbing cock into his mouth, his lips gliding down the rigid length to the black, curly pubic hair at the base. He eased back slightly then plunged forward again, the flat of his tongue laving the underside of the pulsing flesh as he moved up and down on the hard shaft.

A low growl escaped Carlos' lips, and Chris was lifted into the bigger man's arms then gently laid on the bed. Carlos leant over him, his dark eyes locked on those that gazed up at him with longing and trust. Chris raised his head, capturing Carlos with a kiss, moaning softly as he felt the full lips part under his and Carlos' tongue invade his mouth, setting every fibre of every nerve within him on fire. Carlos pulled back a little and began to lick his way over Chris' throat, his chest, his abdomen, into the golden down of his pubic hair. His hands stroked the smaller man's thighs, the tips of his fingers caressed the underside of Chris' balls. He leant forward, taking the head of Chris' cock between his lips, sucking on it smoothly at first then, as Chris writhed beneath him, with long and urgent strokes.

A murmur of ecstasy mixed with some impatience escaped Chris' lips, and he reached for Carlos, tugging at his thigh. "Need that beautiful cock of yours over here." He turned on his side as Carlos shifted position bringing his erection to Chris' eagerly waiting mouth.

"Oh yes," Chris sighed before taking the head of Carlos' throbbing flesh to his lips, licking the tip of the pulsing shaft, savouring the scent and taste of Carlos' arousal. He ran his hand over Carlos' sleek, muscular thighs, explored the cleft between the smooth, round buttocks with his fingers, pushing gently at the ring of puckered muscle he encountered deep inside. He wondered if Carlos would object to his invading this part of him, but as he probed, he heard Carlos sigh with what sounded like appreciation. Encouraged, Chris worked his finger past the slight resistance into the warm, silky tunnel, at the same time sliding his lips over the length of Carlos' hard as steel erection.

Muffled groans came from both men as they pleasured one another, the wet heat of their mouths engulfing each other's cocks, fingers exploring their tight holes and cum-heavy balls.

Carlos pulled away suddenly, and Chris felt a twinge of disappointment but was quickly brought to a soaring ecstasy when Carlos turned him over and thrust his tongue deep inside Chris' stretched opening. He reared up, arching his back, pushing his butt higher while Carlos fucked him with his tongue. Chris thought he might just pass out from this unbearable rapture. Every part of him seemed to glow with a heat he thought might consume him.

"Carlos," he whispered, his voice thick with emotion. "Oh, dear God, Carlos…"

Carlos ran the tip of his tongue up the length of Chris' spine, the head of his cock wedged between Chris' butt cheeks. He reached for a condom from Chris' nightstand and, with one swift motion, sheathed himself then pushed forward into Chris' hot core.

"Close your eyes, *querido*," he murmured into Chris' ear. "Imagine that you and I are soaring through the night sky, just the two of us, you in my arms."

Carlos rolled onto his back, his arms about Chris' chest, their legs intertwined, their bodies fused together. He grasped Chris' erection, pumping it rhythmically in time with the upward thrusts of his hips as he drove himself ever deeper into Chris' silky heat. Chris let himself be caught up in Carlos' fantasy—the two of them, just as they were now, joined at the core of his being, being lifted upwards, out beyond the apartment walls, into the cool night air—soaring, gliding above moonlit clouds. He'd never experienced anything this incredible in his entire life.

He moaned, his hips grinding over Carlos' rock-hard cock, matching the rhythm Carlos had initiated, losing himself in the fantastic vision that unfolded behind his closed eyes. His heart hammered in his chest. He gasped out a choking breath as his orgasm coiled inside him. Ripples of exquisite pleasure raced through him, and he surrendered to the sensation he could no longer control. Crying out Carlos' name, he came, his body shuddering in his lover's arms, as Carlos pumped the cum from him. A second later, his euphoria was intensified when Carlos' powerful body arched under him, climaxing with wrenching, jolting spasms that Chris swore lifted them clear off the bed.

They lay, still locked together, the breath steadying as their bodies calmed. Chris turned his head, seeking a kiss from the lips that nuzzled his earlobe.

"You are sensational, Carlos," he murmured against the soft cushion of Carlos' mouth. "Utterly, totally and mind-blowingly sensational. And how did you do that, exactly?"

"Do what?" Carlos' voice sounded completely innocent.

"You know — that moonlit trip we took."

Carlos chuckled. "I'm glad I have such an unusual effect on you, Christopher. Our imaginations must be in sync."

"And how. Where are you going?" he whined as Carlos disentangled himself from their legs and arms.

"Just to dispose of this." He indicated the used and very full condom.

"Mmm, hurry back." Chris watched with admiration as Carlos strode over to the bathroom, his body a study in classical perfection, every sleek muscle defined in superb detail. Before he could stop himself, Chris let out a low whistle of approval, and Carlos flashed him a stunning smile.

Chris snuggled under the sheet and closed his eyes, his happiness at being with Carlos almost too much bear or to believe. That he could have gotten this lucky, finding someone as fantastic as Carlos, was just unbelievable. And the crazy thing was, he truly felt that Carlos was as into him as he was into Carlos.

He smiled through hooded eyes as Carlos returned, whipped back the sheet and began wiping Chris' chest with a damp cloth. The tenderness in his expression made Chris' heart turn over, and he pulled Carlos down on top of him, holding him as if his life depended on it.

"I love you, Carlos," he whispered and meant every word.

Chapter Five

"I would prefer it if you gave up your position at the Xtasy Club," Carlos said, stroking Chris' hair gently. This was their third night together, and despite the fact Chris had an early morning accountancy exam, he had persuaded Carlos to come over 'just for a little while'. They had made love twice and were now lying snuggled together on Chris' bed, quietly enjoying each other's company.

"Now that you will have a job that pays you handsomely," Carlos continued, "there's no need for you to work at night anymore."

Chris raised his head from Carlos' chest and smiled into his lover's eyes. "We haven't discussed my salary," he said teasingly. "And besides, I should give Lonnie some notice. I can't just call him and say I'm not coming back."

Carlos frowned. "I just don't like the idea of you working there at night. It's not a particularly safe area."

"After what happened the other night, you're right, but the club is only open at night time, so there are no day jobs available. Don't worry..." He kissed Carlos' neck. "I'll give Lonnie a week's notice when I go in tomorrow night."

"Good—and how does a hundred thousand dollars a year sound to you as your starting salary?"

"A hundred thousand dollars?" Chris gasped. "That's far too much, Carlos. I don't even have my degree yet, and—"

Carlos kissed him into silence, holding him pressed tightly to his body. "You will work very hard for your money," he chuckled when he finally released Chris' lips. "I can be a very hard taskmaster.

"Hard is right," Chris remarked as he slipped his hand between their fused bodies and grasped Carlos' erection. "Wow, hard as a rock again. Now what d'you suppose I should do with this?"

"Anything you like," Carlos growled in Chris' ear.

"That's what I hoped you'd say."

* * * *

Feeling a little more confident about the outcome of his exams now they were finally over, Chris entered the back door of the Xtasy Club and made for Lonnie's office. He'd promised Carlos he would give notice tonight and, in truth, was quite relieved to do so. It hadn't been a bad job, and Lonnie had been decent enough, but it was time to move on—and now with

Carlos' offer of a much better position, why should he even hesitate?

"Hey, Lonnie...?" Chris paused at the club owner's office door. "Speak to you for a minute?"

"Sure, kid. Come on in."

"Um...I have to give my notice. Would a week be enough?"

"What, you need more dough? Need a raise?"

"No, no. I have another job."

"Oh, okay. Anyone you know to take over?"

Chris hadn't thought about that. Maybe one of the guys in his class would like the job. "I'll ask around. Is a week enough?"

"Sure, sure, no problem. Just see if you can find somebody to take over. Save me advertising."

"Okay, thanks Lonnie." He made his way down the corridor to his office then decided he'd like a soda. He walked through the already crowded club to the bar, and that's when he saw him—the red haired guy he'd sprayed with pepper the night Carlos had saved his ass in the alley. What the hell was he doing in here? Surely, he wasn't *gay*. The man's eyes met Chris', and his face darkened with rage. Chris felt a shiver run up his back. The moron was out to get him—right here in the bar. What was he? Nuts? Chris changed direction and headed for the exit where Joe, the security guard sat. Joe was a six-foot-seven African American, weighing close to three hundred pounds of solid bone and muscle. Nobody fooled with Joe or even talked back to him—except Paulo, his five-foot-seven, one-hundred-forty pound, Hispanic boyfriend who could deliver a tongue lashing like no one else. But then,

Chris had heard Paulo's tongue was talented in other ways, too.

"Joe." Chris looked up at the giant black man. "One of the guys who tried to beat me up a few nights ago is in the club. I think he's looking for another chance."

"Oh, is he?" Joe's voice rumbled out from his huge chest. "Point him out, sweet chops, and I'll take care of him."

"The guy there by the bar with the red hair."

"Okay, leave him to me." Joe marched his massive frame over to where 'Red' was lurking by the bar. Chris watched as Joe tapped the guy on the shoulder, leant over him and said a few words that had 'Red' taking several steps back and nearly falling over his own feet in his haste to get out of the club.

He scowled as he passed Chris. "You're gonna get yours, faggot," he snarled into Chris' face.

"I said, out!" Joe barked behind him, and the guy scuttled through the door like his tail was on fire.

"Thanks, Joe." Chris smiled at the bouncer. "Can't imagine what he thought he was doing in here. A gay-basher in a gay bar. What's that about?"

"He's lookin' for trouble," Joe growled. "You better get a cab home tonight—and this time, have it pick you up right outside the club!"

Chris nodded, got his soda from the bar then went back to his office where he knew Lenny would have left a ton of work for him to plough through. Joe was right, he needed to take a cab tonight. No doubt 'Red' had something ugly on his mind. Chris couldn't imagine Red's other two friends would be with him. Surely their bones wouldn't have knitted this quickly.

But he might have managed to drum up some other morons to help him 'get the fag'.

Four hours later, he took a break, poured himself a cup of coffee and walked back into the club. His heart lifted when he saw Carlos' tall figure standing at the bar, looking so handsome in a long, black leather coat. Chris' toes curled just from the sight of him.

"Carlos, hi." Chris smiled up at him. "You looking for someone?"

The tall man returned his smile. "Yes, and I think I just found him." He leant in to kiss Chris' lips. "Are you almost through for the night?"

"Yes, but one of those guys who attacked me in the alley was here earlier. Joe says I should get a cab."

"A good thing I'm here then. I don't think the little man will want to take on two of us."

"He might have reinforcements."

"That won't help him."

"Are you sure? I can call for a cab, Carlos."

"Don't bother. We will be quite safe."

After seeing the ease with which Carlos had handled the thugs before, Chris had no reason to doubt what Carlos had just said. Still he felt just a little uneasy.

"You're worried," Carlos said, stroking his cheek. "Don't be—"

"Okay. Just give me a few minutes to clear up the mess in the office, and I'll be right with you."

* * * *

They stepped out into the alley, leaving the noise and the warmth of the club behind. Chris slipped his hand inside Carlos' as they walked towards the busy street at the end of the alley. He couldn't help glancing left and right as they walked and his feeling of unease increased. Carlos' cool hand tightened on his reassuringly, and Chris told himself to relax. Nothing was going to happen.

"Faggots!"

Chris felt the blood drain from his face at the sound of the ugly word rasping from an even uglier voice. Ahead of them, several men stepped out from the shadows of a warehouse entrance.

Jesus. What? They needed an army? Chris' eyes widened when he saw one of the morons carried a gun.

"Carlos," he whispered, "he's armed."

"I see it," Carlos said, his eyes narrowing as the men spread out around them. It was obvious they'd been warned that Carlos was a fighter. There was wariness in the men's stance, a seeming awareness of the tall man's speed and prowess.

"You!" The one carrying the gun gestured at Carlos, pointing the weapon at his chest. "Stand over there while the guys take care of your little buddy."

"No." Carlos' voice was calm as he put an arm around Chris and pulled him to his side. "I gave your friends one fair warning, as I now give you the same. Leave here at once, and none of you will be harmed."

The gunman sniggered. "Ooh, you're really scary." His face twisted as he raised the gun towards Carlos' face. "Now, I don't tell you again. Get out of the way, or I'll shoot."

Carlos moved so fast to Chris it was no more than a blur, but the gunman screamed as the gun disappeared from his hand and he was sent spinning into the two men standing behind him. All three crashed to the ground, and Chris, for the first time, saw 'Red'. The creep had been skulking behind the others and now yelled, "Get them!"

One of the men scrambled for the gun, but Carlos reached down and grabbed him by the collar, swinging him effortlessly off his feet and straight into the warehouse's brick wall. The man went down without a sound and didn't even try to get up, but someone else had grabbed the gun and pointed it shakily at Carlos.

"Get back," the man croaked, more than just a little fear in his voice. The first three men Carlos had laid out were on their feet again and, with murderous expressions, advanced on him and Chris.

"Shoot the son-of-a-bitch!" the redhead howled.

A low growl that made the hair on the back of Chris' neck stand on end escaped Carlos' lips. He lunged forward, the one holding the gun fired, and Carlos staggered back.

"No!" Chris screamed, but to his complete amazement, Carlos did not fall, instead he lunged again, lifted the terrified gunman over his head and flung him deep into the darkness of the alley.

"Holy Christ! What are you?" The man who had confronted them first stared at Carlos, sheer terror in his eyes.

Chris looked up at Carlos and gasped. His lover's face was contorted into a mask of savagery, his lips pulled back, exposing his teeth. Teeth that were very white—and very long and *sharp*.

"*Carlos...*"

His face once more composed, Carlos gazed down at Chris' stricken expression and reached for him, but Chris shrank back against the wall.

"Get them, now!"

Through the turmoil in his mind, Chris was only vaguely aware of the chaos around him. Shouts and screams filled the air. He heard the sound of a shot. He was flung backwards from the impact of something slamming into him then a sharp burning pain filled his body. He felt strong arms enfold him, the sensation of his feet leaving the ground then nothing.

Chapter Six

Carlos gently pushed back the hair from Chris' sweat-covered forehead and bent to kiss his lips. Beside him, Marcus put a hand on his friend's shoulder.

"You must act now, Carlos, if you are to save him."

"I do not intend to change him, Marcus. I simply want to save his life."

"Then do it, quickly," Marcus urged him. "You have removed the bullet. Now give him the blood that will heal his wound."

Carlos grimaced as he remembered those last few moments in the alley. How foolish he had been to expose himself to the men who'd threatened Chris. Because of his arrogance, and his need to terrify the men into submission, Chris had been shot and very seriously wounded. He would not die, but the bullet had severed several nerves in his shoulder. No doubt his right arm would be paralysed if Carlos did not do what Marcus advised.

He took the knife Marcus held out to him and cut deeply into his left wrist. He held the dripping wound over Chris' damaged shoulder, letting his blood flow over the torn flesh, nerves and tendons. Marcus gave a long sigh of satisfaction as the wound began to mend, and the skin closed over the once gaping hole. Once he was satisfied that not even a scar would remain, he held his wrist to Chris' lips.

"Drink," he murmured. "Drink, my love, and be made whole again." He smiled as Chris' tongue licked tentatively at the blood then as the spicy sweetness covered his taste buds, he began to gulp at the life-giving liquid.

"Is that a good idea?" Roger, who had been watching quietly by Marcus' side, asked.

"It will speed the healing," Marcus replied. "Carlos doesn't want Christopher to have any knowledge of what took place."

"But he's going to remember the guys attacking them, isn't he?"

"Yes, but not that Carlos flew him here after dealing with the cowards."

Roger nodded, satisfied with Marcus' explanation.

Carlos eased his wrist from Chris' lips then kissed him tenderly. He looked up at Roger. "Nor that he saw me as I really am." He shook his head with frustration. "My poor judgement put his life in jeopardy. He wanted to call a cab to pick us up at the club. He had seen one of the thugs at the bar earlier and had guessed the man was out for revenge. But I wanted to show him I could protect him. My hubris brought him this pain."

"Hey, don't beat yourself up, Carlos," Roger said, rubbing the other man's shoulder. "Chris is gonna be all right, and all he'll remember is that you saved him from those morons — again."

"Yes, but if I hadn't interfered with his plan to call a taxi, none of this would have been necessary. That bullet could have entered his heart..." Carlos shuddered at the thought. "Perhaps it would be better if I erased all memories of myself from his mind — if I tried to forget what we almost had."

"There you go again, just like Andorra said," Roger sighed. "You give up too easily, big guy. It's pretty obvious to me and Marcus that you love this mortal man — so give it a chance. Don't blow it because of one little setback."

Marcus chuckled and ruffled Roger's hair. "You'd better listen to Roger, Carlos, or *he* won't let you forget the mortal."

"Right." Roger slipped an arm around his lover's waist as he continued. "Marcus here tried threatening me with that little ploy early on in our relationship, and no way would I allow it. I'll bet if you asked Chris what he thought of that idea, he'd use some words that might surprise you!"

Carlos smiled at him. "You are a most unusual vampire, Roger, but I will take your advice, for the time being. It's just that I can still see the expression of horror on his face when he realised what I was."

Roger shook his head. "Well, of course, he didn't realise you are vampire. Most people don't believe we exist. Until I met Marcus even *I* didn't, and I was a horror movie freak—still am. I just hoped you guys *were* out there somewhere. But that's the part you can erase from his mind. All he'll remember is you saved him, and he'll love you even more because of it."

"Well, I thank you both for letting me bring him here." Carlos said. "Now perhaps I had better take him to his apartment before he wakes up."

"And perhaps you can bring him back as a guest on a more appropriate occasion," Marcus suggested. "That is, if you decide to continue your relationship with him."

Before Carlos could reply, Roger said fiercely, "You better not dump this guy, Carlos. It's totally obvious to me and Marcus that you love him."

"*Roger.*" Marcus threw his lover a warning glance.

"That's all right, Marcus," Carlos said, lifting Chris into his arms. "As I said before Roger, I will listen to your advice. Now I should go. I will spend some time with Christopher when he regains consciousness, but I'll be back before dawn—perhaps sooner if he throws me out," he added, chuckling.

"That is not gonna happen," Roger growled. "Love him good, and he'll be yours forever."

* * * *

Chris woke slowly, aware of two things—he wasn't in the alley, and he had a splitting headache. He peered into the darkness of his bedroom.

"Carlos?"

"I am here, Christopher."

"What happened? Why are you sitting in the dark?" He switched on his bedside lamp, blinking as the sudden brightness flooded the room.

Carlos rose from the chair he'd been sitting in and smiled down at Chris. "I was waiting for you to awaken. One of the thugs dealt you a nasty blow to your head." He sat on the edge of the bed. "How do you feel?"

"Like somebody hit me on the head." He reached up to touch Carlos' face. "There were so many of them. Did you...?"

Carlos nodded. "Like all cowards, they ran when confronted by someone who is not afraid of them."

"One of them had a gun." Chris' eyes widened as he remembered. "He shot you, but..."

"Fortunately for me, he missed," Carlos said.

"He did? Well, of course he did, or you wouldn't be here now. Good thing he was such a lousy shot."

"I must apologise to you," Carlos said quietly, stroking Chris' cheek. "If I had listened to you and let you order a cab, this would not have happened."

"But you couldn't have known they'd be out there."

"After you told me about the red-haired one being in the bar, I guessed he would be there with reinforcements, but you see, Christopher, I wanted you to know that I would do anything to protect you. My foolish pride in wanting to act the macho man for you put you in danger. I am so very sorry."

Chris took Carlos' hand and brought it to his lips. "You have nothing to be sorry for. Without you, those men would have most likely killed me. If not tonight, then some other night when I'd let my guard down. I thank you, again, for saving me." He smiled shyly up at Carlos. "And just so you know, I really like that you want to protect me."

Their lips met in a kiss so rapturous Chris felt as if every part of him, body and soul, had been captured and held in that long searing union of flesh on flesh. As Carlos gathered him in his arms, Chris' mind exulted with the thought that everything he'd ever wanted was right here, embodied in this one man. His headache suddenly gone, he felt an erotic vitality course through his body.

Wow, he thought, *what this guy does to me. I might have been laid out in the alley earlier, now I feel like I could take on all those guys by myself — well, maybe with Carlos by my side.* The thought made him chuckle against Carlos' lips, who drew back slightly to squint at him.

"You are amused?"

"Only by my own stupid thoughts." Chris kissed Carlos quickly. "You hold me and kiss me, and I feel like I could take on anyone who gets in my way. I had a vision of you and me knocking the shit out of those guys in the alley."

"I believe you could do just that," Carlos murmured, his lips brushing Chris'. "You are stronger than you think."

"I sure feel it right now." Chris grinned as he flexed the muscles in his arms. "It must be something you've done to me." He tugged at Carlos' shirt. "You gonna get nekkid and get in this bed with me?"

"Your wish is my command." Carlos stood and stripped off his shirt, exposing his magnificently sculpted chest to Chris' admiring gaze.

"Jeez, but you're hot," he whispered, raising himself to a kneeling position on the bed so he could wrap his arms around Carlos' waist and nuzzle the smooth, hard flesh with his lips. He licked his way from Carlos' navel up the centre of his hard torso to his left nipple. He took the tiny nub between his teeth and nipped at it before laving it with his tongue. Carlos' body tensed and shuddered from the sensation, encouraging Chris to trail his lips across Carlos' smooth chest to take the other already hard nipple between his lips and tease it with the tip of his tongue. Carlos' arms tightened around him then he was lying on his back, Carlos leaning over him, the beauty of his body filling Chris with a desire so intense it was almost a hunger. Shaken by the need he felt coursing through him, Chris' startled gaze met Carlos' dark, lust-filled eyes. As one, they moved together, their mouths meeting and blending. With low moans of longing, lips parted, tongues searched and caressed, overwhelming both men with the urgency to claim one another, to possess and mark the other as his own.

Carlos' eyes burned fever bright as the craving for Chris' blood became almost uncontrollable. His lips moved to Chris' throat. The sweet aroma of rich, young blood filled his nostrils, inflamed his senses. The vampire's primal need to satisfy his hunger ripped through him. His fangs extended.

No!

With a guttural cry, he tore himself from the young man's arms, turning quickly away so that Chris could not see the tortured expression on his face.

"What's wrong?" Chris reached out to grip Carlos' biceps. "What did I do?"

"Nothing." Carlos let the hunger ease from him before he could bear to look at Chris. "I am sorry, *querido*," he said quietly, touching Chris' worried face with his fingertips. "I'm afraid my emotions were running a little high. I was afraid I would hurt you."

"Hurt me?" Chris took Carlos' hand and pressed his lips into the palm. "I would never believe that to be possible. " He turned a trusting gaze on Carlos. "You would never hurt me."

Calmer now, Carlos pulled Chris into his arms and kissed his lips gently. The blood lust had receded from him, leaving him with a longing to simply hold Chris, to caress the smooth skin under his hands and to make love to him all through the night.

Chapter Six

Frank Sanders couldn't forget the humiliation that had been heaped on him and his friends the night before. It had been bad enough the first time when the kid had sprayed that goddamn pepper in his eyes. That had hurt like hell for hours. Just as well he'd managed to get away before the cops had shown up.

Well, he was going to get those faggots if it was the last thing he ever did. No way was a pair of pansies going to get away with beating him at his own game—*no fucking way*! And what the hell had Billy been ranting about? The idiot yelling that the big guy was some kind of monster with sharp teeth. What a dickhead. Frank hadn't seen any sharp teeth. All he'd seen was the big guy kicking the crap out of five of his buddies, guys he'd always considered tough—until last night.

Well, he sure as hell couldn't rely on them anymore on account of two of them had concussion, one a broken collarbone, and they weren't exactly thrilled at the way things had gone down. He just wished he could remember exactly what had happened at the end. Try as might, the last few seconds of the fight were a blur. He remembered a gunshot—two in fact. The first one he could have sworn hit the big guy right in the chest, but there had been no blood so he couldn't have been hit, right? The second shot had hit the kid. He was sure of that—or was he? If he'd been hit, how had he gotten away? How had they *both* gotten away?

Damn, but he just couldn't remember.

"Fuck it," he snarled under his breath. He was going to have to think up some other way of getting at those fags. Chances were the big guy couldn't be with the kid all the time. They had to work, didn't they? And he knew where the kid worked. All he had to do was make sure that huge security guy didn't see him. He'd recognise him for sure—Frank's red hair was a little hard to miss. Well, he'd think of something, and when he did, both those cocksuckers were going to pay—big time!

* * * *

Chris did a happy dance after he put down the phone. The mechanic at the service station had called to say his car was finally ready for him to pick up. Yeah! Now he didn't have to worry about getting to and from the club at night, even if Carlos wasn't around to escort him up the alley—although he had already decided that wasn't going to happen again. He'd told Carlos next time—a cab. Only now, it would be his own car, and besides, he just had five more nights to work there.

"Which reminds me," he muttered. He had to remember to ask around if anyone wanted the job. Maybe Joey? But he really didn't want his friend working in that dump, and maybe running into that red-haired jerk and his friends.

Man, you'd think after Carlos had beaten the shit out of them — twice — they'd give it up!

He smiled as he thought of Carlos and how wonderful their night together had been. It all seemed to just get better and better. Even the trauma in the alley couldn't get in the way of their lovemaking. As scared to death as he'd been when he'd seen one of those guys carried a gun, all of it, and them, was forgotten when Carlos held him in his arms and kissed him with such incredible passion.

And last night had been different somehow. After Carlos had recovered from whatever had brought about his fear of hurting Chris — how could too much passion have hurt him? — it had been wonderful, but *different*, in a way he couldn't quite fathom, almost as if *he* himself had been different. The physical side of their lovemaking had been spectacular every time. Carlos was a consummate lover, passionate, yet tender, demanding, yet giving, and always infinitely loving. Chris had never known anyone remotely like him, had never experienced such a tidal wave of sensuous emotion — and last night, all of it, every kiss, every caress, had been even more fantastic, if that were possible.

The memory of their time together had Chris getting hard. He was just about to stroke himself when the shrilling of his cell phone brought him from his sensual reverie with a jolt. Oops, his mother.

"Hi, Mom."

"Hello, Chris. How are you?"

"Fine."

"How did the exams go?"

"Pretty good, I think. I should have the results next week. Oh and I'm getting my car back today."

"Good, that means you can drive up to see us this weekend."

"Uh, I might have plans."

"You *do* have plans, Christopher."

Oh, oh. *Christopher.* Now he knew she was upset. Funny how the way she said it was so different from when Carlos did. He said it like a caress; his mother more like an accusation.

"I do?"

"You're coming home to visit your mother and father," his mother said tartly. "We haven't seen you in over two months, and your father wants to talk to you about setting up an office for you here for when you do our accounts."

"Oh, about that—" Wait, he couldn't just tell her about his job offer from Carlos over the phone. "Okay, Mom." He hoped she hadn't heard the long sigh he'd just heaved. "I'll see you and Dad Saturday morning."

"That's better. We do miss you, you know?"

"Miss you too, Mom. See you on Saturday."

Chris put the phone down with a feeling of irritation. True, Carlos hadn't said anything about getting together over the weekend. Chris had just assumed they would. Now instead, he'd have to drive to Santa Barbara and face his parents' disappointment when he told them about his job offer. He could just imagine the opposition and the questions.

Who is this person? How did you meet him? How do you know he's legit?

I don't know, Mom and Dad. I just feel that he's an honest man. But what's more important, he's terrific in bed, and I can't wait to spend every night right there with him.

Yeah, that would go down a treat.

Heaving another sigh, he punched in his friend Joey's number. "Hey, Joey—wanna take a trip with me this weekend?"

* * * *

Carlos awoke from the deep sleep of the vampire, instantly aware that Chris needed to talk with him. Covering his nakedness with a robe of dark-red silk, he picked up the phone by his bed and dialled Chris' number.

"Hello, Christopher. It's Carlos."

"Hi!" The genuine pleasure in Chris' voice made Carlos smile. "I was just thinking of you," Chris said in a rush. "I don't know if you had plans for the weekend, but I've been summoned to my folks' place in Santa Barbara, so I'm afraid I'll be out of town for a couple of days. I hope you don't mind."

"Of course not." Carlos quickly hid his feeling of deep disappointment so that it was not reflected in his voice. "Although I have to admit I will miss you, very much."

"And I'll miss you, Carlos. My mom insisted I come up. They want to talk to me about putting an office somewhere in the house for me—you know, for when

I do their accounts. I'm still trying to think of a way to tell them I'll be working for you, so they won't be upset."

"Ah, there is no need to upset them. The work I will have for you can be done in a few hours a day. There will still be time for you to take care of their business."

"But they'll want me to move back home."

Carlos smiled as he heard a distinct whine creep into Chris' tone. "That is something you must work out with them," he said quietly. "I'm sure you can persuade them that with today's technology, most everything can be conducted via the internet."

Chris managed a light laugh. "That's a good point, but you don't know my mom. She hates the fact I live in LA. I'm taking my friend Joey with me for moral support. They've known him since we were in junior high together, and he can be very persuasive—especially with my mother. She thinks the sun shines out of his ass—not that she'd put it quite that way, but you know what I mean."

"I think so."

"So can I see you tonight? I'm not working."

"Yes, if you don't mind meeting a few friends of mine. We're having a glass of wine at a little restaurant on Santa Monica—La Fortuna. Do you know it?"

"Uh, yeah," Chris replied. "I know where it is. Your friends won't mind?"

"Not at all. Shall I pick you up at your apartment, at say, eight o'clock?"

"That'd be great. See you then."

"*Hasta la noche*—until tonight."

Carlos put the phone down and wondered if what he had just done was a wise move. Obviously, if his relationship with Christopher was to continue — and he wanted that very much – then he would have to be included in some aspects of Carlos' life. There was no need for Chris to know everything, not yet at any rate, and Carlos could be certain of his friends' discretion. Ron, Jean-Claude's lover and the manager of La Fortuna, was still mortal, yet they had a successful and committed relationship, despite Ron's brother and *his* lover's tendency to arrive on Ron's doorstep from Portland without warning.

It could be done, with care, and although it would be so much easier if Christopher actually knew the truth, why should he be burdened with such an enormity? Vampirism, as seen through the human psyche, was enough to make the strongest man or woman run in terror. No, it was not yet time for the truth. And again, Carlos chastised himself for almost losing control and letting the bloodlust take over. He shuddered as he thought of the consequences had he not fought it with every vestige of his will.

Never could he allow that to happen again.

Hearing the sounds of murmured voices in the house, he stood and made his way downstairs to find Roger and Marcus in the living room, side by side on one of the couches, discussing something they had seen in the newspaper. Marcus looked up and smiled as Carlos entered the room.

"Hey, Carlos—" Roger waved the newspaper at him. "Get a load of this. Some guy swears he was attacked by a vampire the other night."

Carlos took the newspaper and quickly scanned the article, sighing with some relief as he read the last lines. *"Although Billy Richards swore he was not hallucinating, the police have put little credence to his statement, as no one else involved in the fracas saw anything strange about their attacker. The men described their assailant as extremely tall – close to seven feet, one said, and weighing about three hundred pounds.* Nothing strange indeed," Carlos chuckled.

"Well, they wouldn't want to sound like a bunch of wimps," Roger pointed out, winking at Carlos. "I mean anyone who could actually lay out six men at once had to be huge – or a *vampire.*"

"I thought I had cleared their minds of the moment I revealed myself," Carlos said, frowning. "Obviously I missed this one."

"Or he had some form of immunity against mind control," Marcus suggested. "We know there are certain humans who cannot be influenced by us – fortunately, a very few."

"Well, the police think he's looney-toons," Roger remarked airily, "so I wouldn't worry about it." He rose from the couch. "I'm going to get ready for our night out."

"I hope you don't mind." Carlos touched Roger's arm. "I invited Christopher to join us at La Fortuna tonight."

"Wow." Roger beamed at him. "This *is* getting serious."

"So Roger, try to be low key, please," Marcus warned him. "I'm sure Carlos doesn't want his date scared off by any of your of-the-wall remarks."

Roger put his hands on his hips and tried to look offended. *"Well*, I would never try to spoil Carlos' date. I shall be the soul of tact, as always." Carlos and Marcus looked at one another and smiled. Roger narrowed his eyes at Marcus. "You, on the other hand, Mister, will have to do without later tonight."

"Without what?" Marcus asked innocently.

"You know what—what you crave from me incessantly!"

Marcus raised one perfectly shaped eyebrow "That's funny. I could swear it was the other way round."

"Huh!" For once, Roger seemed stuck for a comeback. Instead, he flounced towards the living room door with a, "Get ready, you two," command that left Marcus chuckling.

"I've said it before," Carlos remarked, watching Roger's exit, "but he is one of the most unusual vampires I've ever met."

"Roger is a one off, for certain," Marcus agreed.

"And he was mortal when you met."

"Yes."

"And how were you going to cope with that, if your ex-lover, Thomas, and the Comte hadn't interfered and necessitated him being changed?"

"We had talked about it," Marcus said. "I had laid out the options for him. Just like Andorra's blood gives Tony a longer life, so it could have been with Roger and me." He gave Carlos a knowing look. "So it could be with you and the mortal of your choice. If he is, of course, willing."

"Yes, I have thought of that." Carlos smiled as he remembered. "He responded, uh…very well to my blood the other night."

"Well…" Marcus chuckled softly. "Before you make any decision, see how he responds to meeting your friends tonight."

"Should I be concerned?"

Marcus raised an eyebrow. "Roger will be there."

"Ah."

Chapter Seven

Ron Hendricks, the manager of La Fortuna and lover of vampire Jean-Claude Lepeltier, took a look round his empty restaurant and sighed with relief. The last of his customers had just left, and now, he could set up a table for his late night guests. A corner table, out of sight from those passing the restaurant's window was already occupied by Jean-Claude. The slim and elegant Frenchman smiled at Ron as he hurried over carrying a tray of wine glasses.

"Relax, *mon cher*," he said, taking a couple of the glasses from the tray and placing them on the table. "It will be a few more minutes before they arrive— time for us to enjoy a glass of wine, alone together."

Ron leant in for a kiss from his lover. "That sounds good. I brought a bottle of your favourite Pinot Noir up from the cellar." Ron had long since explained these late night gatherings to the restaurant's owner as a small club of wine connoisseurs. The owner, delighted with the extra revenue and the fact that Ron took care of it himself and had no need to pay any of the staff overtime had brought in some speciality wines for the 'club' to sample. If he wondered why all the white wines were ignored, he did not ask why.

"You could always tell him we're the Red Wine Society if he asks," Roger had suggested. "You know, like the Red Hat one."

Ron smiled as he thought of Roger and Marcus and the others, and of how much his life had been changed since meeting Jean-Claude. Not as much as his friend Micah's had been, he reflected with a wry twist to his lips. Ron was still a mortal, though destined to live longer than the normal span of human life, due to the occasional infusion of Jean-Claude's blood. But Micah had made the decision to join Joseph in immortality after he and his lover, Joseph, had both narrowly escaped death at the hands of an evil vampire and a crazed demon.

A tap at the door broke into his thoughts.

"They're early," he said to Jean-Claude, pulling the cork from the bottle of Pinot Noir. "Could you let them in?"

"Of course." Jean-Claude squeezed Ron's arm as he passed him on his way to the door. "Don't be alarmed, but I think we have a mortal visitor."

"Who?" Ron fell quiet as Jean-Claude opened the door and admitted Carlos and a young stranger. *Oh boy*, he thought gloomily. *It's gonna be a 'pretend night'.* Ron had, over the course of his relationship with Jean-Claude, been able to tell vampire from mortal at a glance. Some vampires, such as Jean-Claude himself, Marcus and Roger, could pass for mortal without difficulty, while others had an ethereal quality that set them apart and made them easy for him to recognise. Ron had not met Carlos before this evening, but he knew immediately who he was. Roger had called ahead to let him know to expect their friend from Spain. Ron also knew that the young man accompanying Carlos was most definitely not vampire.

He sighed as he thought of the side-steps everyone would have to take to keep him ignorant of the fact that the man he was dating was an immortal—that was exactly why he never invited Jonas, his brother, to these get-togethers when he was in town. Jonas would freak if he ever found out Jean-Claude was vampire. Ron's lips twisted in a wry smile. *Actually, freak wasn't a strong enough word.*

He pushed those thoughts aside as he went to meet Carlos and his friend.

"Ron..." Jean-Claude smiled at him as he introduced Carlos. "This is our friend from Spain, Carlos Galeano. Carlos, my lover, Ron Hendricks."

Carlos took Ron's hand in both of his and bowed slightly. "My pleasure, Ron. Roger has told me what a good friend you are to him. I believe you have had some adventures together."

Ron grinned, charmed by Carlos' gracious manners. "Life's never dull when Roger's around."

"And this is Christopher Jeffries," Carlos said, taking Chris' arm.

"Hi." Chris took Ron's proffered hand with a shy smile. "Thanks for inviting me."

"Oh, you're welcome. I've just opened a Pinot Noir," Ron told Chris. "The guys are all red wine drinkers, but I have beer if you'd rather?"

"Red wine's great," Chris said quickly.

Carlos took Chris' hand as Jean-Claude led them to the corner table. "Christopher's parents own a vineyard in Santa Barbara."

"Wow." Ron sounded impressed. "Hope this Pinot Noir passes muster." He put a glass in front of Chris and poured a small amount of the dark-red liquid. "I'll let the expert be the judge."

"I wouldn't say I'm an expert," Chris mumbled, raising the glass to his lips. He took a small sip, savouring the wine on his tongue before swallowing. "Very nice."

Jean-Claude patted Chris' shoulder. "You have good taste. That is my favourite."

A loud rapping at the door had Ron chuckling. "That'll be Roger." He ran to the door and flung it open.

Chris stared, startled, as a blond-haired young man threw himself into Ron's arms and started to chew on his neck — or at least, that's what it looked like from where Chris was sitting. He felt a rush of relief when Ron laughed and disentangled himself from the young man's arms and legs.

"Roger, you really are too much."

"Better than not being enough," the one called Roger replied then cast a long look towards the table where Chris sat. "You must be Chris...topher," he said, advancing on the table, all smiles.

"R-right." Although not tall, Roger had a larger than life appearance that made Chris slightly nervous. As his hand was taken in Roger's cool grip, Chris couldn't help but notice the man who loomed over Roger's shoulder was, without doubt, the most beautiful man he had ever seen in his entire life. He found himself almost mesmerised by the emerald-green eyes that twinkled at him from a face that could only be described as perfect.

Roger caught Chris' expression and grinned at him, showing very white teeth. "This ugly guy is Marcus, and I'm Roger. Pleased to meet you."

Chris shook hands with them both, wondering if any other corner table in LA could boast so many hot-looking men. And it wasn't over yet. Ron answered the door again and admitted two more handsome strangers introduced to Chris as Joseph Meyer and Micah Fitzgerald.

How many more hotties are going to show up? he wondered.

"That's it, no more," Roger said, smiling at him. "The gang's all here."

Chris stared at him. *Did he just read my mind?* "Did you just read my mind?"

Roger chuckled. "Yes. Didn't Carlos tell you I moonlight as a clairvoyant?"

Good-natured laugher rippled round the table, but Carlos didn't miss the warning look Marcus cast at Roger. It seemed that Roger's impishness could get a little out of hand at times.

"Christopher is from Santa Barbara," Jean-Claude said, changing the subject from things paranormal.

"Nice," Micah remarked. "A bit conservative though."

"Tell me," Chris laughed. "West Hollywood's at the opposite end of the spectrum in comparison."

Ron brought another bottle of wine to the table. "This vintage has passed inspection by Christopher who is heir to a vineyard in Santa Barbara."

"Wow, impressive." Roger held out his glass for a refill. "What label should we look for?"

"Mountain Ridge Fine Wines," Chris replied, a trace of pride in his voice. "The cabernet won honourable mention in *Great Wines Magazine* last year."

"I'll tell the boss to order some for the bar," Ron said. "He's always looking for new brands."

"I'm going home for the weekend, so I'll bring a bottle for you and him to sample." Chris looked around the table at the handsome men and found himself relaxing in their company. He'd been a little nervous of meeting Carlos' friends, but they seemed so nice and friendly. He couldn't help but notice how bonded the couples were. If Micah sat any closer to Joseph, his lover, he'd be in his lap, while Ron and Jean-Claude traded small smiles with one another across the table. Roger was a kidder, but easy to like, and Marcus — well, his sexy smile and husky voice would turn anyone's head — even Chris' — if he wasn't already smitten with Carlos. He turned to smile at the man in question and took his hand.

Funny, that his hands were always so cool to the touch, and now, when he thought about it, all the men he'd shaken hands with had that same coolness — all except Ron whose hands had been as warm as his own. Strange… He was suddenly aware Roger gazed at him with mischievous eyes.

"Cold hands, warm hearts," Roger murmured.

"You did it again," Chris exclaimed. "How do you do that?"

Roger's expression changed to one of innocence. "Do what?"

"You read my mind, again. You weren't kidding when you said you were clairvoyant, were you?"

"*Roger*." Marcus made an imperceptible movement with his hand, and Chris laughed suddenly.

"That's the darnedest thing." He flushed slightly with embarrassment. "I've totally forgotten what we were talking about. I'm sorry."

"You were telling us about the cabernet from your vineyard," Joseph said, leaning forward with seeming interest.

"Oh right. Well, it's not mine. I mean, it's my parents' vineyard, but I'm very proud of what they've done." He wondered why Marcus was looking daggers at Roger, not that Roger seemed worried about it. He was smiling sweetly at Marcus who gave a loud sigh of resignation. Well, he must have missed something there, he guessed.

Chris leant back in his chair as Carlos massaged the back of his neck with his strong fingers. Oh, but that felt good. The sensations rippling through his body created in him a need to be alone with Carlos, to show him just how much he loved him, and would miss him while he was in Santa Barbara.

Carlos put his lips to Chris' ear and whispered, "We won't stay long. I have a need to be alone with you."

Chris felt his cock harden as Carlos' lips lingered on his ear after echoing his own thoughts. If it wouldn't have appeared rude, he'd have jumped to his feet right there and then and dragged Carlos out of the restaurant without so much as an apology. But that *would* be rude.

He tried to concentrate on the conversation that surrounded him like waves of sound then Roger's voice broke through the laughter. "Hey, Chris. You like horror movies? I got the DVD of *Van Helsing* — you know the one with Hugh Jackman? It's worth it just to watch him."

"Oh yeah, I liked that one." Chris smiled at Roger. "You're right. Hugh's the man."

"That's for sure," Micah agreed. "I wouldn't mind seeing that one again."

"And again," Roger said, grinning. "Okay, our place next week. What night's good for you, Chris?"

"Uh, well I should be back from Santa Barbara Sunday night, and my last night at the Xtasy is Tuesday, so…after that maybe?"

"Then let's say Wednesday night. Micah can pick you up if you like."

"That's okay, I have wheels, and Carlos can give me directions."

"Are we all to have this movie inflicted upon us?" Marcus asked pointedly. "Joseph isn't keen on that type of entertainment."

"And neither are you, I know." Roger was still smiling at his lover. "You're both such sticks-in-the-mud. Just because you're older than God…" His voice trailed off, and he looked around the table with a guilty expression on his face.

Chris said nothing though he found Roger's remark a little strange. Marcus and Joseph looked to be only in their late twenties, if that. He must have meant that they had old-fashioned tastes or something.

Carlos broke the awkward silence by standing and holding out his hand to Chris. "I think perhaps we should go. Christopher has an early start to his day tomorrow."

"Right." Chris got up and smiled at the others. "It was really nice meeting you all."

"Don't forget about next Wednesday." Roger seemed to have regained his composure as he grinned up at Chris. "Around eight, okay? I'll have some stuff to nibble on."

"Look forward to it." Chris let himself be led from the table, his hand in Carlos' firm grasp.

Ron walked them to the door. "Nice meeting you both." He put a hand on Chris' shoulder. "Stop in any time you like. I won't make the Hugh Jackman party, I'm afraid. I work nights."

"Oh, that's too bad." Chris said. "Are you open for lunch?"

"Uh, yeah..." Ron and Carlos exchanged glances. "But, uh, dinner's a better idea."

"Okay, we'll figure something out. Nice meeting you, Ron."

* * * *

Ron closed and locked the door behind them then walked slowly back to the table where he knew Roger was in the dog house. *Man, but he just can't control his mouth sometimes.* As he thought, Roger was looking downcast and apologising to Marcus and Joseph. Joseph seemed okay with it, but Marcus was definitely over Roger's big mouth.

"Before we left the house tonight, I asked you to be careful what you said in front of Christopher, and you immediately made a show of reading his mind and telling him what he was thinking! Roger, you cannot do this around mortals." Marcus looked over at Ron as he took a seat at the table. "Except Ron, of course — and Tony. And besides, it's rude to read other people's minds unless there is a good reason for it."

"I'm sorry," Roger said, sighing. "I guess my sense of humour is not always appropriate."

Micah laughed lightly. "I think Christopher is going to be puzzling over that remark you made about Marcus and Joseph being older than God."

"Thanks for reminding me." Roger sighed again, louder this time.

Marcus smiled and shook his head. "Your melodramatic sighing won't get you off the hook that easily. Just make sure that the next time you meet Christopher you avoid throwing around any more clues as to what we are."

"I was just kidding, you know," Roger protested. "And besides, the last thing on Chris' mind right now is that he might be going home with a vampire."

Marcus chuckled and cuffed Roger lightly on the back of his head. "Nevertheless, I don't want to see a look of abject terror on the young man's face if he ever should work it out from your sometimes very pointed remarks. Letting him know you can read his mind for instance. A slip of the tongue is one thing, but deliberately coming out with some of those off-the-wall comments like you did tonight is not a good idea. Do you think you could control your teasing for a few hours next time Christopher is around?"

"Yes," Joseph said, trying to look affronted. "Like saying Marcus and I were older than God!"

"You guys are no fun," Roger pouted.

Micah chuckled at Roger's gloomy expression. "But you have to admit they make up for it in lots of other ways."

Chapter Eight

Frank stared at his friend Billy Richards like he was sporting five heads. "Are you totally out of your freakin' mind? A fuckin' vampire? There's no such thing, Billy. Look at me. Listen to me. *There's no such fuckin' thing!*"

"I'm telling you what I saw," Billy snapped. "That guy had fangs as big as a tiger's — and not only that, his face was like, *contorted*, somehow. Not human."

"You're nuts," Frank sneered. "What the hell were you on, for Chrissakes?"

"Listen, Frank." Billy raised a warning hand near Frank's face. "Don't go tellin' me I'm nuts. I know what I saw. And what about when Whitey shot him? That bullet hit him right in the middle of his chest. It hardly fazed him. Made him stagger some is all. Then he was all over us again. I'm telling you, the guy's not human — not real."

"Oh, for fuck's sake." Frank turned away from his friend in disgust. "Horseshit, Billy, just plain horseshit. Whitey missed the son-of-a-bitch, that's all."

"Okay, fine, you don't believe me."

"Of course, I don't believe you. I was there and so were Fred and Whitey and those other two morons you brought along. We didn't see no vampire, Billy. All's I saw was some dude beating the shit outta you and your pals."

"Vampires can make you forget things."

"What now?"

Billy locked eyes with Frank. "I read about it," he said quietly. "About *them*. They have the power to get into your mind and fuck with your brain."

"What brain?" Frank sniggered. "You go around talkin' like this, you'll end up in the looney-bin with all those other freaks. I mean, I can't believe you told the cops that story. It's amazing they didn't cart you off to a freakin' asylum."

"Very funny, Frank." Billy eyed his friend coldly. "Well, let me tell you this, just so you won't be able to say I didn't want to cut you in on the deal."

"What deal?"

"The deal about finding the vampire and exposing him for what he is."

Frank's cackle caused Billy to grind his teeth in anger.

"For what he is, Billy?" Frank sniggered. "He's a man, that's all. A homo who's got the kind of smart moves you and your moron friends couldn't compete with. Look, I'm gonna get the son-of-a-bitch, and if you want to put a stake through his heart to satisfy some freaky fetish you've got going, that's fine—but you'll have to wait 'til after I put a bullet in his brain."

"Just make sure it's a silver bullet."

"Oh, for fuck's sake, Billy." Frank ran a hand through his rufus-red hair. "You are really getting on my nerves with this crap."

Billy shrugged. "D'you realise how much money we could make if we could bring in a live vampire? We'd be famous Frank. We'd be on every talk show in the US. Even Oprah!"

Frank stared at his friend for a long moment then rolled his eyes and shook his head. "A live vampire? Vampires are supposed to be dead people walking, Billy. They're not *alive*. They come out of graves."

"No, that's not true. See, I read about this—"

"You, *read*? When did that happen?"

"Cut it out, Frank." Billy was anxious to share what he'd read. "There's this breed of vampire that lives just like we do, 'cept they can't be out in daylight, and of course, they have to drink blood. But they don't sleep in coffins like in the movies, and you wouldn't really know what they are just by lookin' at them."

Frank tapped his fingers irritably on the arm of his chair. "Billy, even you have to see this is bullshit. Some stupid, new-age baloney you've been readin'. Some asshole out there is tryin' to make a fast buck by writin' this crap, and stupid jerks like you lap it up. Shit, I could write something that stupid."

Billy decided to let that one pass. "Frank, just hear me out. These vampires can be captured. They can be tied up with silver chains. It weakens them, and they can't snap the chains."

"And where d'you suppose you'll find a silver chain? I don't think they're talkin' the kind that goes round you girlfriend's neck like that cheap-ass necklace you bought her. They probably mean heavy links." Frank giggled. "And then what happens? You go near him, and he'll take a chunk outta your neck."

"I'm telling you, the silver weakens them so they can't hurt you, and they can't fly away."

Frank laughed so hard he thought he might bust a gut. "*Fly away*? Oh, Billy you surely are one stupid motherfucker. It's just as well there's no such thing as a vampire, or you would be one drained asshole by now!"

He was still laughing when Billy got up and slammed the door on his way out.

"Dumb shithead," Frank muttered, glaring at the door Billy had almost taken off the hinges. "*Vampires.* Jesus, he'll be seeing werewolves next. Stupid asshole."

* * * *

Chris pulled his Camaro into the parking lot of the 7-11 and grinned at Joey. "So, just some coffee?"

"Yeah, black, sweet and strong." Joey yawned then sighed. "You got me up so darned early this morning I didn't have time to get my morning caffeine injection."

"Be right back."

"That's okay. I'll come in with you. I can use the restroom while you order."

They were on their way to Santa Barbara, and Chris was really glad he'd convinced his friend to join him for the weekend. Of course, he thought rather uncharitably, he would have preferred it if Carlos could have come with him, but he had another of those pressing business appointments—even on a Saturday. Still, it might be just a little early to be introducing him to his mom and dad. They weren't going to be that crazy about him hooking up with a guy—especially one he'd met in LA. They were still getting used to the fact he was gay. Joey, they liked, but that was because they saw him as Chris' best friend from junior high days. They'd known him since he was a kid, and sure didn't know anything about the mad sex fiend he'd grown up to be.

Boy, Chris thought, *if I'd have brought home just ten percent of the guys Joey's dated to meet my folks they'd have had a shit fit!*

He carried their coffees outside and waited for Joey by the car. The warm sun felt good on his bare arms and legs. Warm days, cooler nights and now that they were approaching Halloween, longer nights.

He smiled as Joey bounced out of the 7-11. With his tousled, chestnut curls framing a cute face, twinkling blue eyes and a perpetual sunny smile, Joey was a target for just about every gay man he met. Only recently had he started to get picky about whom he went out with. It was a sign of maturity he'd told Chris, giving them both a good laugh.

"Hope your mom is cooking breakfast when we get there," he said, accepting his coffee from Chris. He glanced at his watch. "Nine o'clock. We should be there in another hour, right?"

"Right, but forget breakfast, they'll have been up since six. She'll make us a sandwich or somethin'."

"So, you going to tell her you're dating?" Joey asked as they got back on the road.

"No. Mom and Dad don't really want to hear that just yet."

"But they're gonna have to get used to the idea one of these days. I mean, Chris, you're twenty-four years old, not their little baby anymore."

"Try telling my mother that."

"I will."

"No, you won't. Joey, don't even bring up the subject, please. I'll tell them when I know what's happening with Carlos and me. He's offered me a job."

"*Has* he now? So tell me, what's he like?"

"Beautiful, Joey, just so amazingly hot. I couldn't believe he was giving me the time of day."

Joey chuckled. "Well, you're not exactly a troll, Chris."

"Gee, thanks for that."

"No, I mean, you think I'd run around with some dweeb?" Joey grinned at him. "I have a reputation to maintain you know."

"Hah, some reputation. The tramp of the class of '02."

"I could take exception to that remark—if it wasn't true!" Joey laughed out loud. "Oh God, those were the days. We had fun, right?"

Chris grinned at his friend. "Yes, we did, though I think you had more than your fair share."

"Tell me. Anyway, we got off the subject of Carlos. How hot is he? Describe him for me."

"Well, he's tall, about six-four, I'd say."

"Mmm…"

"Thick, black hair."

"Oh, I like him already. Tall, dark and handsome."

"Dark-brown eyes with flecks of gold."

"I'm gettin' hard—"

"Stop that, you." Chris chuckled. "He's built too, great body."

"Big cock?"

"Joey!"

"Well, he can't be all of the above and hung like a mouse."

"I can assure you he's not hung like a mouse."

"Aha. No wonder you're looking so damned self-satisfied."

"Joey, there's more to him than just his good looks. He's so great, so *caring*, in and out of bed. "

"Oh *my*…" Joey poked Chris in the ribs. "Ah do declare, mah best fren's in *love*."

"Yes." Chris stared straight ahead as he said, "I do believe I am."

* * * *

Their weekend with Chris' parents' wasn't quite the chore Chris had thought it might be. Chris loved his parents, and even if his mother could be a bit of a control freak at times, he knew her actions and thoughts were for his well being. Having Joey there with him had been a good idea. His mom loved Joey, regardless of how outrageous he could be at times. She even let him call her by her first name, Anita. So, it was easy for Chris to sometimes drift from the conversation at hand and let his mind linger on the last wonderful time he'd spent with Carlos. He just had to be careful when he stood up since thoughts of Carlos invariably made him hard. The tenting in his jeans or shorts was not something he wanted his mother to catch sight of.

However, he knew that getting across the idea to his parents of him doing their accounting from anywhere else other than right there in the winery wasn't going to be easy. His dad might see it was possible, but his mother just would not understand why he'd want to do such a thing as stay in LA.

"That immoral, dangerous place..." she'd railed at him on several occasions, and this time she had a newspaper article to show him, to prove to him that LA was the last place on earth he should want to live.

"And that goes for you too, Joey," she exclaimed as she thrust the paper under Chris' nose. "I immediately thought of the danger you could both be in when I read that."

Sighing, Chris scanned the article with the lurid headline *Vampire Attack in Los Angeles*.

"Mom, why on earth are you reading this kind of crap?" he groused. "This is like something out of one of those tabloids you get at the supermarket checkout."

"Maybe so," his mother said with a sniff. "But the man swears it's true."

Chris read out loud for Joey's amusement. "*Billy Richards, arrested after a fracas in a West Hollywood alleyway, gave police some startling details of the man he says attacked him. Richards admitted he and his friends had planned on mugging two men in the alley, but the taller of the two suddenly grew in height and revealed sharp fangs as he defended himself and his companion.*

"'It was like something out of a horror movie,' Richards declared. 'The guy was close to seven feet tall and could toss all of us around like we weighed nothing. Even a bullet in the chest didn't stop him. And he had fangs, terrible long teeth.' Richards and two others were fined for carrying a weapon without a license.

"The incident took place a short distance from the Xtasy Club, a bar generally frequented by gays."

"Hey," Joey exclaimed. "Isn't that where you—?"

"No!" Chris almost yelled. "It's not the same place." He glared at Joey, signalling that his friend shouldn't say another word in front of his mother.

"The same place?" Chris' mother stared at her son. "What does that mean?"

"Nothing."

"You're not going to those awful places are you?"

Chris sighed. There was no point in trying to hide it from her. She'd harp on it until he came clean. "I was working there as their bookkeeper, but I've given them notice."

"Oh Chris, why would you work in a place like that? If you needed extra money, your father or I would send it to you. You know that."

"Mom, please. I'm twenty-four years old. I can't be asking my parents for money all the time. That's why I got the job—so I could pay my bills without bothering you or Dad."

"Well…" His mother smiled benignly. "I suppose that's very thoughtful of you, but I'd rather you asked us instead of working in some sleazy bar."

Chris couldn't really defend the Xtasy Club's reputation without hearing a hoot of derisive laughter from Joey so he didn't bother. Instead, he decided to broach the subject of his working for Carlos—and staying in LA.

"Talking of work," he began, "I've had a pretty good job offer from a guy who deals in the international antique business."

"But you'll be working for your father, *here*," Anita said pointedly.

"Well actually, I want to talk to you and Dad about that."

"About what?" his father asked as he entered the living room.

"Chris has been offered a job," his mother interjected before Chris could say anything. "He seems to have forgotten his obligation to you, Jack."

"Mom, please. Let me explain how this can work."

"Go ahead, son," his father said, easing himself into his favourite armchair.

"I met this man—his name is Carlos Galeano— through mutual friends." Mentally, Chris crossed his fingers as he told this little lie. He was not about to say he'd met Carlos in the alley outside the Xtasy Club! "He imports and exports antiques. His business is based in Madrid."

"Madrid?" His mother looked at him aghast. "You'd be going to Madrid?"

"No, Mom, I'd be doing the accounting here in the States, on a computer programme I'll set up with his help. I've already mentioned to him that you expected me to do the winery accounts, and he said that wouldn't be a problem. It can all be done on the internet."

"Can it, Jack?" Anita looked at her husband for clarification.

Jack nodded. "Sure it can, but it's going to be a load on you, Chris. Two accounting jobs? And the import-export market can be volatile at times. You'd be taking on a lot, son."

"I'd like to try it though, Dad, if it's okay with you."

Jack was about to nod his assent when Anita jumped in again. "Well, if it's so easy to do all that on the internet, why can't you do it from here? You'd have your own office, and you'd be home."

Joey and Chris exchanged glances then Joey said, "Oh, Anita, you'd be taking my best buddy away from me. I'd be all lonesome in the big, bad city!"

Anita gave him a narrow-eyed look. "You should come home too, Joey. Your mother worries about you being down there, just like I do."

Jack Jeffries let out a long, low chuckle. "They're not mamma's boys, Anita. They're young men needing their own lives. I'm sure Chris can share his time here and in LA."

Chris felt a huge surge of relief at this father's words. *Good old Dad—always ready to come up with a compromise.*

"I can do that," he said eagerly. "I'll talk to Mr. Galeano about it. I'm sure he won't mind."

"This Mr. Galeano…" Anita was not so easily persuaded. "What do you know about him, exactly?"

Chris ignored Joey's muffled snort. "He's a very successful, sophisticated kind of a guy. You'd like him, Mom."

"Then perhaps you should bring him here so we can meet him."

"Sure." Chris smiled sweetly at his mother. "I can do that."

* * * *

Later, lying in their separate beds in Chris' old room, Chris had to listen to Joey's criticism on how he'd handled the situation.

"You should've told them right there and then that Carlos was your boyfriend," he hissed into the darkness of the room.

"I don't know that he is my boyfriend, yet."

Joey sighed loudly. "Well, when *are* you going to know? I let a guy fuck me more than once, he's my boyfriend!"

Chris chuckled. "Well, we can't all live by your high standards, Joey dear."

"Watch it," Joey growled, then giggled. "That was a bit whorey, wasn't it?"

"I miss him already," Chris whispered, more to himself than Joey.

"Poor baby. Want some company over there?"

"No thanks. And Joey, if you have to jack off, please don't mess up the sheets. My mother still checks for tell-tale signs like that."

"Anita loves me, and she'll understand."

"Oh, boy."

After Joey had fallen asleep, Chris lay awake for some time, thinking about the article he'd read about the attack in the alley. Of course, he knew the piece had been about the guys who'd tried to put Carlos down, and who had failed miserably in the attempt. Their story, in order to justify the whipping Carlos had given them made him smile. They couldn't just say they'd been beaten by a better and stronger man.

No, they had to make up some cockamamie story about Carlos having fangs and being seven-feet tall.

Jeez, what losers.

* * * *

He was in a long, dark and deserted alleyway. No matter how fast he walked, ran even, the end of the alley seemed nowhere in sight. He could hear his heaving breath, feel his heart pound in his chest and a film of cold sweat coated his skin.

He knew he was being followed, and he knew danger lurked ahead. Which one to face? Either way, the odds were insurmountable. Alone, he couldn't take on the three men who now stepped out of the shadows in front of him. If he ran, he would have to face whoever was behind him. Three or one? He turned and ran straight into the strong arms of a tall man wearing a long, dark coat.

Chris looked up, and his heart leapt with exhilaration. "Carlos," he murmured. "Oh, thank God."

"You're safe now," Carlos whispered. "Safe, my love."

The three men snarled their defiance and charged forward, clubs and knives raised to strike and slash. Carlos plunged in among them, hurling their bodies away with superhuman ease. But the men returned, time and time again. They would fall, hit the ground then rise again. One loomed behind Carlos, knife raised to stab him between his shoulder blades. Chris screamed out a warning, and Carlos turned and — oh God, what had happened to his face?

His features, usually so handsome, serene and composed, had taken on the likeness of a monster — eyes blazing with a murderous fury, lips drawn back in a hideous grimace to expose long, sharp fangs. The man who would have stabbed him now shrieked with terror as Carlos picked him up bodily, and with one ferocious bite, ripped out his throat.

Chris stared with terror, bile flooding his mouth. He let out a long cry of horror.

* * * *

Carlos, sitting alone in the guest bedroom of his friends' home, reading a book, was startled at the sound of Chris' despair piercing his awareness. He reached out with his thoughts, his mind closing the distance that separated him from Chris.

A dream — or rather a nightmare — that's what it was, he thought, his mind calm now once he knew Chris was not in any immediate danger.

A dream, my love, just a dream. I am here with you. You are safe, querido mio.

He heard Chris whimper in his sleep then felt his mind clear itself of the ghastly images the nightmare had brought him. For a moment, Carlos was tempted to go to him then rational thought took over. He consoled himself with the knowledge that Chris would be back in LA the following evening, and he had every intention of seeing him then.

Satisfied that Chris would now sleep peacefully, with only pleasant dreams to remember, he settled back in his chair and gave in to the pleasure thoughts of Christopher brought him.

Chapter Nine

Billy Richards was enjoying his fifteen minutes in the limelight. Just that day, he'd had two more publications contact him about his lucky escape from the 'Vampire of West Hollywood' as the *Public Enquirer* had dubbed his attacker. Somehow, the media was focusing less on Billy's role as the potential mugger and more on the lurid details of the man Billy swore was a vampire. And Billy knew he was right. The guy they'd tried to bring down in the alley that night was more than human. His buddy Frank could laugh at him and deride him all he wanted to, but Billy knew what he'd seen, and what he'd seen didn't belong on the streets of the city.

Each time he thought about that night, a few more details gelled in his mind. The kid the monster had been with, the young guy Frank was intent on beating the crap out of, the one who worked at the faggot bar, how did he figure in all of this? He had to have known what the big guy was. According to Frank, it was the second time he'd accompanied the kid down the alley. They were buddies, no doubt about it. Which meant, in fag terms, they fucked around.

The kid had to know what it was he was in bed with, for Chrissakes.

He was probably letting the vampire drink his blood. Humans did that.

Ever since the incident, Billy had been doing some serious reading about vampires, even struggling through Bram Stoker's *Dracula*. Buffy was a much easier read, he'd decided.

In the process he'd learned that vampires befriended humans who gave their blood willingly. Little sips now and then just to keep their undead buddies going, without being turned into a vampire. Billy shuddered at the thought, but at the same time, he couldn't deny he was kind of intrigued by it. Not the homo part, of course. If he could just find himself some hot chick vampire, he might let her take a bite or two—nothing too deep or too much…

He jumped as his phone rang. "Hello?"he managed after almost dropping the receiver.

"Billy Richards?"

"That's me. Who's this?"

"My name is Martin Van Helsing."

Billy let out a hoot of laughter. "Yeah, and I'm Billy Renfield. What? You've been reading the papers would be my guess."

A deep chuckle sounded on the other end of the line. "*Touché*, Billy. Actually my name is Martin Kellogg— the Van Helsing part is my idea of whimsy. When you hear what I do for a living, you'll understand."

Billy wasn't sure what 'whimsy' was. The guy must be a faggot using words like *touché* and *whimsy*. "And just what is it you do for a living—like I care," Billy rasped.

"I'm a vampire hunter."

Despite himself, a thrill ran up Billy's spine at the man's words. *A vampire hunter.* Of course, if there really were vampires—and he was convinced there were after what he'd seen that night—then there would have to be vampire hunters. Probably working for the government.

"Oh, yeah?" Billy figured the right way to handle this would be to appear nonchalant as possible. The guy could be some kind of kook after all. "How'd you get my number."

"You're listed."

"Oh, right. So, how can I help you?"

"Can we meet, say for a coffee, in about a half hour? There are some details I'd like to get concerning your, uh…confrontation with the vampire."

"What's in it for me?"

Another deep chuckle. "You mean, monetary remuneration?"

"If that means reward, then yeah."

"I'm sure we can come to some satisfactory arrangement."

Billy felt his excitement mount. "Okay, where d'you want to meet?"

* * * *

Chris dropped Joey off at his apartment then headed home. All in all, the trip to Santa Barbara had worked out just fine, he reflected, driving along Santa Monica Boulevard. Clearing the air about working for Carlos had been a good idea, and even if his mother still wasn't crazy about it, she had succumbed in the end to his dad's more easy-going attitude.

He pulled into a parking space outside his apartment building, and his heart raced as he caught sight of a tall, familiar-looking figure standing on the steps outside the front door.

"Carlos!" he shouted happily, grabbing his overnight bag and hurrying from the car. "What a great surprise. How'd you know when I'd be back?"

"A lucky guess," Carlos replied, opening his arms to embrace Chris.

"I missed you," Chris mumbled against Carlos' lips after their first breathless kiss. "Come on in. I've got lots to tell you."

Smiling, Carlos followed Chris up the steps and into his apartment. Chris opened his overnight bag and produced two bottles of wine.

"Ta-da! I got one for Ron to give to the owner of La Fortuna and, this one, this is for us to share. Like some?"

"I would like that very much." Carlos studied the label for a moment. "You must be very proud of your parents' success."

"I am." Chris hurried into the kitchen to get the wine glasses.

"Another special occasion?" Carlos asked, recognising the antique glasses.

Chris smiled shyly. "Every time I'm with you is a special occasion." He uncorked the bottle. "We should let it breathe a little."

Carlos held out his hand. "Then come here so I can thank you for the nice thing you just said."

Chris took his hand and let himself be drawn into Carlos' arms. He sighed happily as he kissed his lover's chin then slid upwards to nibble on his lower lip.

"You are the absolute best," he whispered, pressing against Carlos' hard body.

Their parted lips met, and Chris, consumed by the rapture Carlos brought him, felt himself melting, except for that part of him that grew and hardened at Carlos' touch. Every kiss, every caress from this man brought Chris to the edge of delirium. The taste of his mouth, the sweetness of his breath, the spicy scent of his skin overwhelmed Chris' senses.

He shuddered with anticipation at the sensation of Carlos' lips teasing his nipples through the thin cotton of his tee. Quickly, he peeled it off, wanting the even more sensuous sensation of Carlos' lips and tongue on his bare flesh.

Trembling with pleasure, he fumbled with Carlos' shirt buttons, sliding his hands inside to caress the hard muscle overlain with smooth, cool skin. As their lips meshed again in another long, languorous kiss, Chris' hands roamed over Carlos' back, tracing the length of his spine, slipping under the waistband of his pants. Carlos writhed against him as Chris' fingers probed the cleft between his buttocks.

Carlos popped the metal stud at the waist of Chris' jeans then slowly unzipped the fly, delaying the delicious moment when his hand could enclose Chris' hard cock. Even more slowly, he sank to his knees, his lips trailing an erotic path down Chris' torso until he reached the object of his desire. His tongue flicked at the head, scooping up the pre-cum that oozed from the slit. He paused for a moment, savouring the delicious salty flavour then he eased Chris' jeans down over his hips, cupping the smooth round globes of his butt in his hands. A long, shuddering breath escaped Chris as Carlos' mouth engulfed his throbbing erection, sliding up and down the hard length, from tip to base. Chris' head fell back in ecstasy, his hands clutching at Carlos' hair, his fingers tangling in the thick mane. He groaned, his orgasm building inside him too quickly to control.

"Uh…Carlos. Oh, *God.*"

And Carlos sucked harder, stronger, taking Chris over the edge into a mindless, searing delirium that had him coming in convulsive spasms, filling his lover's mouth with his hot semen. Carlos' eyes smiled up at him as he swallowed it all down, licking away the vestiges that clung to the still sensitive head. Carlos stood, and Chris collapsed into his arms, burying his face against the taller man's hard chest.

"Wow…" The breath from Chris' sigh of satisfaction warmed Carlos' cool skin. He bent slightly to kiss the top of Chris' head then lifted him into his arms and carried him into the bedroom. Laying him on the bed, he pulled off Chris' sandals and jeans, threw his own clothes aside then covered Chris' body with his own. His eyes held a tender light as he gazed down at Chris, smiling gently.

Chris returned his smile shyly. "What's Spanish for I love you?" he asked.

"*Te quiero,*" Carlos replied in a husky whisper.

"Then, *te quiero*, Carlos. *Te quiero* very, very much."

Chris pulled him down for a kiss, their lips parting for each other, their tongues sliding together, filling one another's mouths. Carlos ran a hand down Chris' slim torso, his fingertips gliding over his lover's smooth skin, straying into the musky warmth of his crotch. He slipped his hand under Chris' balls and followed the sensitive, silken path leading to his tight opening. Chris shivered from the sensation and raised his hips slightly, letting Carlos' middle finger probe gently at the puckered hole. Carlos paused for a moment as if remembering something then he smiled, withdrew his hand and reached for the lube and a condom from the nightstand.

Chris wrapped his legs around Carlos' waist, his breath quickening with anticipation as Carlos' lubed finger resumed its probing, easing past Chris' resistance, sliding all the way in. Chris' cock jumped as Carlos pressed against his prostate. A soft whimper escaped his lips. Carlos moved over him, replacing his finger with the head of his now sheathed cock. He pushed forward as Chris pressed down. Low moans of pleasure came from both men as their bodies were joined and they rocked together, Carlos losing himself in the rapture of being inside Chris, surrounded by his heat. Their arms tightened about one another, their lips met and meshed, tongues tangling, teeth clashing as their passion overwhelmed them.

The rhythm they had begun quickened, each thrust from Carlos' powerful hips bringing Chris an ecstasy he had never dreamed of. His cock, trapped between their fused bodies, ached for release, and as he arched his pelvis upward to meet yet another searing thrust, he climaxed with a choking cry, his hot semen coating their torsos.

"*Querido*..." Carlos shuddered in Chris' arms as he came, driving himself even deeper inside Chris, his body racked by spasm after spasm. Chris held him, kissing his chin, his lips, his neck, all the while murmuring words of love and admiration. Carlos rolled over onto his side, his arms still wound around Chris, his eyes glistening with unspoken emotion. Chris laid his head on Carlos' chest and closed his eyes, knowing at that moment, he had never been happier in his entire life.

* * * *

The rail-thin man sitting at a corner table, stared through his dark glasses at the younger man who had just entered the coffee shop. Must be the one, he thought, taking in Billy's attempt to look indifferent as his gaze swept the room. Martin Kellogg raised his hand a fraction then indicated the seat in front of him. Neither man uttered a greeting, just simply stared at one another, assessing strengths and weaknesses.

Finally Martin said, "Disappointed?"

"Yeah." Billy's upper lip twisted a little. "You don't look like a vampire hunter."

Martin chuckled. "But *you* do look like a petty criminal."

"Hey." Billy bristled at the insult. "Watch your mouth."

"Then tell me, Billy. What do you think a vampire hunter should look like?"

"I dunno. FBI agent maybe. Fit, built—you don't look like you could take on a vampire. Especially the one I seen. How do you take them down?"

"I have my methods."

"Silver chains?" Billy asked smugly, wanting Martin to realise he knew a thing or two about vampires.

"That and one or two other means."

"Are there a lot of you guys out there huntin' vamps?"

"Not so many—but then, there aren't that many vampires."

"How many you killed then?"

Martin's thin lips parted in a humourless smile. "I've killed my fair share."

"Really?" Billy was still doubtful. "You're kinda old for this, ain'tcha?"

"Forty—and you are?"

"Twenty-eight."

"Twenty-eight." Martin sighed. "And still out there trying to mug people—and for what purpose? What do you intend your life to be, Billy?"

"What's it to you?" Billy's tone was belligerent. "Just cut to the chase. What do you want, and what's in it for me?"

"Very well." Martin removed his dark glasses, and Billy flinched slightly at the unnerving stare the man levelled at him from pale, cruel eyes. So pale, Billy couldn't even discern what colour they might be. "In one of your statements to the press, you said the vampire was accompanying a young man."

"A fag, yeah. Second time, Frank said."

"Frank?"

"A buddy. He's the one wanted them put down."

"For what reason?"

"They're fags."

"Ah." Martin held Billy's gaze until the younger man looked away. "So, this was intended to be a gay-bashing exercise, not a robbery."

"Well, we'd take what they had as well," Billy mumbled.

"So, the young man with the vampire—who is he?"

Billy shrugged. "I dunno his name. Blond kid, pretty-boy type. He works at the Xtasy Club is all I know."

"I see. And this club is where?"

"I don't know the *address*. I could show you where it is—just don't ask me to go in. I don't want no fags comin' on to me."

Martin smiled thinly. "Somehow, I don't think you'd have to worry about that."

Billy's hands curled into fists on the table top. "What's that supposed to mean?"

"What it means, dear Billy, is that you would look out of place in a gay bar, and gays have a nose for those who don't belong."

"Are you sayin' *you* belong?" Billy pushed his chair back slightly, leaning as far away as he could from Martin.

Martin's sigh was heavy. "No, I'm not saying that. What I'm saying is I wouldn't enter a gay establishment with hatred flashing from my eyes. I would try to blend."

Billy snorted with disgust. "Well, you can blend all you like. Leave me out of it."

"With pleasure. Tomorrow night, you will show me the place, and I'll take care of the rest."

"What are you going to do?"

"I'm going to make the acquaintance of the vampire's mortal friend, of course," Martin replied with a smirk. "If, as you say, they are more than mere friends, what better way to bring the vampire from his nest?"

"And what do I get from all this?"

Martin's smile did not warm his pale eyes. "That depends on the degree of success we have, Billy." He replaced his dark glasses and rose from the table. "I'll be in touch. Be ready when I call."

Once outside, Martin walked quickly away from the coffee shop. It was as he had feared. Billy would be of no use to him, other than guiding him to where the vampire's young friend was employed. Martin had guessed from the newspaper article that Billy was an opportunist but had hoped he might at least have had some of the qualities needed for a vampire hunt. This would be the first time Martin would work solo. At first, it had seemed like a good idea — collect the bounty without having to share with a partner, but now he was not so sure. If only Billy had shown more strength of character, he might have been able to use him and offer him a fraction of what a real partner would expect for his share. But Billy had the typical limited intelligence of the petty thief and criminal and could not be trusted.

He mounted the steps to the small room he had rented for the duration of his stay in Los Angeles. There had been a time when he could have afforded more luxurious accommodations, but his admitted gambling addiction had recently decimated his bank account, forcing him to sell his car in order to pay off some of his Vegas creditors.

It had been a stroke of luck that he had read Billy's story and recognised it as no hallucination, but a real vampire sighting. Such sightings were rare enough, and he wanted to waste as little time as possible in determining the vampire's whereabouts before some other eager hunter contacted Billy. The story was just bizarre enough to make the national press then it would be a race against time — and the competition.

Martin opened his leather satchel and took stock of its contents, nodding with satisfaction on seeing everything he would need to arm himself against the vampire when the time came. He pulled out one of the silver knives, his hand trembling slightly as he grasped the ebony hilt. This had been his father's but had not been handed down to Martin willingly. Even now, after all these years, a quiet rage filled Martin as he remembered the old man's contemptuous words after his failed attempt to capture and kill the Spanish vampire they had tracked for over a month. It would have been Martin's first kill, and despite his lengthy training under his father's, at times, cruel training, Martin had not sufficiently gauged the vampire's incredible strength and speed — nor his ferociousness when cornered.

Martin had felt real terror when faced by the snarling creature, and even his father's shouted assurances that the sun would soon be up and the vampire would weaken did not stop him from stumbling backwards in fear, knocking his father over in his attempt to dodge the vampire's outstretched hands. It was fortunate that the vampire was more intent in escaping the sun's rays than in killing either Martin or his father, and had raced for the comparative safety of a nearby forest's shade.

Listening to his father's tirade of blame as they'd unsuccessfully tried to track down the vampire had filled Martin with shame and the determination to quit the old man's authority. He had returned to the States alone, had sought out the covert association that paid bounty for a captive or dead vampire, and had been partnered with Vince LaGuardia. Well built, handsome, and with a superior manner that intimidated Martin, LaGuardia proved to be a coolly efficient hunter with several kills to his credit, mostly in Asia and Africa.

"Vampires living in the US are harder to locate," he told Martin. "They've managed to blend in better in the big cities, especially when they have mortal lovers – although at times, that can be their weakness. Gay or straight, vamps can't seem to resist a mortal's company."

Martin was going to use that weakness now to corner his first solo kill. And despite the nervousness he couldn't quite shake off, he was so ready to tell Vince of his success — and to tell him to go to hell. Vince's arrogance had grated on Martin's nerves from the beginning. It would be the greatest pleasure to tell Vince he didn't need him anymore. He couldn't wait to see the look on Vince's face when he showed him the bounty he'd collected — all by himself. Yes, that would make it all worthwhile — that, and the bounty, of course.

Chapter Ten

Chris was not looking forward to returning to the Xtasy Club. Even the knowledge he only had a couple more nights to work there couldn't make him feel better about it. But he had promised Lonnie, and Carlos had said he'd be there before the end of his shift. *At least, they wouldn't have to walk up that damned alley*, Chris thought smugly. He had his car back.

The club was busy when Chris arrived. Some young guys were celebrating a birthday in one corner. They'd hired a stripper for the birthday boy, and the whooping and hollering was reaching ear-splitting level. Chris had to close the office door so he could concentrate on the work that had piled up over his days off. After a couple of hours, he ambled over to the bar for a cup of coffee to have with the sandwich he'd brought. As his eyes swept across the crowded club, he was momentarily startled by the long stare of a man sitting at the far end of the bar. The man's unswerving gaze was fixed steadily on Chris, a slight smile on his thin, pale face.

Chris shivered and a prickle of unease ran down his spine. Was the guy hitting on him? Not to appear rude, Chris gave him a watery smile then turned away to pour his coffee. Joe, the bouncer on duty, clapped him on the shoulder.

"I hear it's your last night tomorrow," he said, his lips close to Chris' ear so he could be heard above the noise. "We'll miss you, Chris."

"Thanks, Joe." He gave the big man a quick smile.

"I would say come back 'n see us, but I reckon this isn't really your kind of place."

"Not really, but maybe I could meet you and Paulo for coffee somewhere."

"That'd be good." Joe gave him a hug, and Chris disappeared briefly in Joe's massive arms.

"Who's the strange guy at the end of the bar?" Chris asked, taking a quick peek round Joe's broad shoulder.

Joe turned to look then shrugged. "Who?"

The man had gone, and Chris felt a rush of relief, though he was not quite sure why. "Oh, some guy was staring at me. Guess he's gone."

"Lots o' guys stare at you, sweet chops." He swatted Chris' behind, and Chris laughed, wading through the crowd, carrying his coffee carefully on the way back to the office. He stopped short when he saw the man who had been staring at him, standing at the office door in an obvious attempt to speak to him.

Chris tried to ease his way past the man. "Can I help you?"

The man turned his pale-eyed gaze on Chris and smiled. "I think perhaps the question should be, can I help *you*?"

"Excuse me?" Again, Chris tried to get past, but the tall, thin man effectively blocked his way. "Look, do you mind? I have work to do here."

"So do I," the man murmured, pushing Chris into the office.

"Hey, what the —?"

The office door was slammed shut behind them. "You don't know, do you?"

"Know what?" A shudder ran down Chris' spine as he stared into the man's cold eyes. "Who are you? What do you want?"

"My name is Martin Kellogg, but who I am is of no consequence. What I want, is another matter, however. What I want is your vampire friend."

Chris barked out a short, surprised laugh. "Are you nuts? I don't have any vampire friends. There's no such thing as a vampire. Oh wait, you read that stupid article in the paper, didn't you? Surely, you don't think what that idiot told the reporters is true."

Martin's humourless smile thinned his lips. "Oh, I can assure you there are such things as vampires. Not only that, I can tell you have been tainted by vampire blood."

"*What?*" Chris stared at Martin, now thoroughly convinced he was talking to a madman.

"Is he coming here tonight?" Martin asked, his eyes narrowing to mere slits. "You will bring him in here."

Chris took a step back, wondering how in hell he could get out of the office. He could yell, but with the noise outside in the club, no one would hear him. The guy was obviously nuts, but there was something else about him—something cruel and dangerous. Chris had a feeling that Martin Kellogg would have no compunction whatsoever about hurting him, badly. There was just one chance—and Chris took it. With one quick motion, he hurled the contents of his coffee cup into Martin's face. The coffee wasn't hot enough to scald, but it had the desired effect of taking Martin by surprise. With an involuntary cry of surprise, he reeled back, covering his face with his hands, and that was enough for Chris to dart through the office door.

"*Joe,*" he yelled, running as fast as he could towards the bouncer's station by the main entrance. "There's some crazy guy in the office!"

Joe left his station at the door and strode over to the office with remarkable speed for someone his size. "Nobody here, Chris," he boomed, peering inside.

Chris joined him in the office. "He was here, Joe. I threw my coffee at him." He pointed at the Styrofoam cup and the spilled coffee on the floor. "He was talking crazy about me having a vampire friend and about my blood being tainted. He had to be nuts."

Joe shook his big head slowly. "Nutcases everywhere these days, sweet chops," he said. "He must have gone out the emergency exit. I told Lonnie to get that stupid alarm fixed."

"Well, thanks anyway, Joe." Chris stooped to pick up the coffee cup. "I'll get a rag and clean up this mess."

* * * *

Martin walked quickly into the shadows outside the club, wiping furiously at his face. That damned kid would pay for making him look stupid, he seethed.

"What happened?" Billy stared at Martin's wet face. "Where's the kid?"

"In the club," Martin snarled, unwilling to inform Billy of how Chris had outsmarted him.

"You smell like coffee," Billy said, sniffing at Martin. "Hey, your shirt's all wet." He snickered loudly. "What—the kid got the better of you? The fearless vampire hunter? What a loser!"

Martin's right hand shot out and grasped Billy by the throat. "Shut your stupid mouth," he growled, "or that insult will be the last thing you ever say."

Billy's eyes bugged in his head, and he squirmed in Martin's vice-like grip. "Aaah, lemme go, you moron," he squeaked.

Martin relaxed his hold on Billy's neck but did not release him. He pulled him in close until their faces almost touched. "I suffered a setback tonight," he hissed. "Don't compound my anger by uttering asinine remarks, or your services will be dispensed with. Do you understand?"

Billy quaked as he gauged the thin man's strength to be out of proportion to his appearance. He nodded his understanding then staggered back as Martin released him.

"The boy doesn't know what his friend is nor is he in the vampire's thrall." Martin eyed Billy keenly. "Do you understand what I'm saying?'

"Yeah, I read about it. It's when the vampire kinda has you hypnotised so you'll do what he wants."

"Mmm. Except it is much more than that." Martin's pale eyes gleamed in the darkness. "Much more. The vampire can bend your will, make you forget what he doesn't want you to remember—make you go to him, willingly, whenever he calls."

Billy shuddered. "You mean he could make me...*want* him?"

Martin's smile was closer to a sneer as he stared at Billy. "Again, I don't think that is something you should worry about."

* * * *

Carlos flew swiftly through the night sky, his mind consumed by thoughts that all was not well with Christopher. He had said he would meet him at the end of his shift, but moments ago, he had felt Chris' panic and, after a quick explanation to Marcus and Roger, had left their company to make sure he was all right. Alighting gently in the alleyway, he strode quickly to the Xtasy entrance. He gave Joe the bouncer a brief nod as he entered the club.

"Is Christopher still here?" he asked.

"Sure is—and he'll be glad to see *you*," Joe replied, putting a meaty hand on Carlos' shoulder. "Some dude was here talkin' crazy crap 'bout vampires and such."

Carlos stiffened. "Vampires? Did you see this man?"

"No, he took off after Chris doused him with his coffee." Joe chuckled. "Got some spunk, that kid."

Carlos walked quickly to the office and tapped on the door.

"Who's there?"

"Christopher, it's me, Carlos,"

"Oh, Carlos…" Chris unlocked the door and pulled Carlos inside. "Boy, am I glad to see you." He threw himself into the bigger man's arms and held him tight.

"Joe told me what happened," Carlos whispered, stroking Chris' hair gently.

"I couldn't believe it, Carlos. The guy was nuts. Had these really nasty, pale eyes that seemed to look right through me."

Pale eyes. "Did he say his name?" Carlos asked quietly.

"Yeah. Martin something. Kellogg—Martin Kellogg. But what was crazy, he asked me if my vampire friend was coming here tonight! I mean, *vampire*, for Pete's sake."

Carlos tightened his arms about Chris and kissed his forehead. "The man was obviously insane," he murmured. With a finger under Chris' chin, he tilted his face to his own and brushed his lips tenderly. "I think you should call it a night and let me buy you a drink."

"That's the best thing I've heard all day." Chris smiled into Carlos' eyes. "Thank goodness tomorrow's my last night here. Won't have to deal with any more fruitcakes talking about vampires!"

"Hmm…" Carlos leant back a little and winked at Chris. "I think your personal bodyguard will make it a point to be here during your whole shift tomorrow night."

Chris chuckled. "And afterwards?"

"That, too. I'm afraid you might get rather tired of me hanging around."

"I doubt that very much." He snuggled deeper into Carlos' embrace. "If I lived forever, I would never tire of you."

Carlos rested his chin on top of Chris' head, gently smoothing the curls through his fingers. "Even if you lived forever?" he asked softly.

"Even then," Chris replied.

* * * *

"We have a vampire hunter among us," Carlos told Marcus and Roger later that night. After he had seen Chris safely home, had made love to him then made sure he was soundly asleep, he had waited in the dark outside the apartment just in case the hunter lurked nearby. At last, satisfied that they had not been followed, he returned to his friend's home in the Hills.

Marcus stared at him silently for a moment or two then asked, "Are you certain?"

Carlos nodded. "His name is Martin Kellogg. The same Martin Kellogg involved in the near death of my friend Juan Ramirez two years ago. Juan described him as reed thin with pale eyes. Tonight, he visited Christopher at the club. He described him to me in much the same way."

"Wow." Roger leant forward in his seat. "Chris? Is he okay? Where is he?"

"He's at home, quite safe. I made sure we were not followed."

"You should've brought him here," Roger said.

"I think that might have presented too many problems, Roger."

"Carlos is right." Marcus, a study in panther-like grace, rose from the couch and walked over to the bar. He poured Carlos a glass of wine. "He can watch over him from here. Now that Christopher is imbued with Carlos' blood, they are more closely attuned than before."

"Right," Roger grunted. "But this hunter guy. How much of a threat is he?"

Carlos grimaced as he accepted the glass of wine from Marcus. "He could be a very real threat. The fact that he confronted Christopher tells me he wanted to use him as bait. He actually asked if his 'vampire friend' would be meeting him at the club. Of course, Christopher thought him insane and told him so."

"How'd Chris get away?'

"He threw a cup of coffee into the man's face and bolted out the door."

Roger howled. "Oh man, wish I'd been there to see that!"

"So do I, Roger." Carlos sipped his wine slowly then stared moodily into the dark-red liquid. "I have a boundless hatred for vampire hunters."

Marcus squeezed Roger's shoulder. "Carlos' lover, Miguel, was murdered by vampire hunters," he said quietly.

"Oh, I'm sorry, Carlos."

Carlos smiled sadly at the young vampire. "It was many years ago, but vampire hunters pass their skill and lore onto their descendants. I intend to find out if Kellogg's ancestors were Miguel's murderers."

Roger was wide-eyed with interest. "How would you find that out?

"By questioning him once I have him in my grasp."

"Is that wise, Carlos?" Marcus asked. "Would it not be better just to dispose of him quickly and quietly?"

"I intend to dispose of him, Marcus, after I have questioned him. If he is indeed the spawn of those murderers then I will feel Miguel's death has been avenged."

Marcus sighed. "If that is your wish."

Carlos ground his teeth in frustration. "All these years, Marcus, I have been tormented by the fact I was unable to slay my lover's murderers. Now, perhaps I can right that wrong." He downed the last of his wine then said, "I will not ask for your help in this. It is my vendetta to carry out alone."

Roger looked at Marcus with concern. "But we have to help him, right?"

"Of course, we will help you, Carlos," Marcus said firmly. "I have already alerted our friends to the hunter's presence. We all need to be vigilant. If he discovers there are several of us here in LA and learns of our whereabouts, he will no doubt call for reinforcements. I imagine he would consider it quite a coup to wipe us all out. Those who fund his operation will most likely increase the bounty he can earn."

"Forgive me." Carlos nodded his acknowledgement of what Marcus had just said. "I was thinking only of my own need for vengeance. Of course, the others must also be informed and protected."

"And Chris," Roger murmured.

Carlos met Roger's gaze and held it. "Most assuredly, Roger. Christopher's safety is of paramount importance to me — and always will be."

* * * *

Alone in his room, Carlos stood by the window, gazing sadly out into the darkness of the early morning. Christopher's confrontation with Martin Kellogg was not something he had foreseen, and it had brought back many unpleasant memories to mar his otherwise newfound optimism. He found his mind slipping back to the fateful day when Miguel had been attacked by vampire hunters — an incident that should never have had the tragic consequences that followed. Ordinarily, Miguel would have been more than a match for the hunters, but he had let down his guard momentarily as he'd walked through the grounds of their home just before dawn.

Carlos knew Miguel enjoyed these moments just before sunrise, staying outside until the first burning rays appeared over the horizon. For that reason, he had not been concerned that Miguel was not always indoors as the day lightened. But on this particular morning, Miguel had been followed from the village by three hunters who had recognised him as a vampire, and were determined to collect the bounty paid for the head of every vampire brought in. These men were generally desperate charlatans, and not beyond cutting off a mortal's head, filing his or her teeth into points to represent fangs, then claiming the bounty. Sometimes the magistrates were foolish enough to believe the ploy, others were not so easily duped.

Then there were the professional hunters, those who knew vampire lore and used it against them. They had planned their attack well, only minutes before sunrise, when a vampire is at his weakest, when his body grows heavy with fatigue and the call of his resting place cannot be ignored. Miguel had fought well, even managing to kill one of the hunters, but as the sun rose, bathing his body in its searing light, his strength had evaporated and he had fallen under the hammer blows the hunters inflicted upon him.

Carlos, already asleep, had been abruptly awakened by the terrible realisation of Miguel's death. He had risen from his bed and rushed to the door, flinging it open, almost blinded by the light, but still able to see the headless and charred remains of his lover lying in the courtyard, only a few feet away. Risking his own flesh being burned, Carlos had dragged Miguel's body inside, had buried him in the vaults below the house and, later, had searched for the men who had taken his reason to live from him.

The hunters had made good use of the daylight hours, putting distance between themselves and any vampire seeking retribution for what they had done. Carlos would have killed them both had he been able to find them. Usually not one for violence against mortals, Carlos nonetheless knew he would feel no remorse for bringing about their deaths. To drain them dry then snap their necks was what he craved night and day. Their escape was not something he could live with easily, for he had been sapped of emotion, emptied of feeling, knowing he would never love as deeply and completely again – until now.

Until Christopher.

Chapter Eleven

Martin Kellogg eyed Billy with contempt. He was sorry now that he'd used this foolish man in any part of his plan to hunt down the vampire. Billy had told his friend Frank about their meeting and had actually brought him along to meet Martin. Frank had stared at him like he was some curiosity, an alien being to be held not in awe but with derision. Frank's sniggering sarcasm had finally sent Martin over the edge, causing him to pull his silver knife from its scabbard inside his coat and hold it under Frank's wobbling Adam's apple. The fool's eyes had stared back at Martin, terror and a desperate need for flight reflected in their watery blueness.

Billy had laughed, quite happy to see his so-called friend recoiling in abject fear.

"Maybe now you'll believe me," he'd taunted Frank. "Not so quick with the put downs now, are ya?"

Martin had sent Frank stumbling away with the warning never to snicker at things of which he had no knowledge. And now he had to deal with Billy who was still voicing glee over his friend's humiliation.

Martin sighed. "Billy, Billy. You really are quite useless to me."

"What d'ya mean?"

"You have no conception of what will be needed when we come face-to-face with the vampire, have you?"

"We? What, there's a mouse in your pocket or something?"

From the less than amicable look Martin threw him, Billy guessed his attempt at humour had fallen flat. *This guy really takes himself way too seriously*, he thought. *And from what I've seen so far he's not too swift. Wonder if he's just full of it – maybe he's never even seen a vampire.*

Martin started to walk away without another word, Billy trotting in his wake. "Wait, where're you goin'?"

"To do something I can better do on my own," Martin said, not looking back at Billy.

"Oh, come on man," Billy whined. "I gotta see how you do this." Then he added as a taunt, "*If* you can do it, that is."

Martin turned so abruptly, Billy all but collided with him. "Listen to me," the hunter hissed, his eyes cold and full of dislike. "Your friend just learned that I have no time for fools. You would do well to remember that, Billy. What I do has inherent dangers and allows no room for mistakes. My biggest mistake would be in having you at my side."

"Hey, wait a minute—"

"You won't have the stomach for it," Martin snapped, resuming his purposeful stride. "You and your ilk are all bluster and no balls."

"Oh yeah? I'm the one who seen the vampire, not you." Billy grabbed at Martin's arm. "You wouldn't have known about it if I hadn't told the press my story."

Martin again stopped dead in his tracks and swung round to face Billy. "And what did you do then, Billy? When you saw him, did you stand your ground, or did you run screaming into the night?"

"Well, I ain't stupid—"

Martin's lips twisted in a wry smile. "So, you ran. Which is why you would be of no use to me."

"Wait," Billy huffed. "I won't run this time. You've got the stuff to stop him, haven't you? The silver chains and knife and all the gear to put him down."

"But I don't have a reliable man at my back," Martin said. "A hunter's partner must have the same resilience and courage as the man he works with. There is no room for error or cowardice. I would rather attempt this on my own than have someone who might run at the first sign of fangs. Go away, Billy. Here—" He dug into his pocket and pulled out some dollar bills. "Take this, and forget about hunting vampires. You'll live longer that way."

Scowling, Billy took the money and stuffed it into his back pocket. He watched as Martin turned on his heel and strode off along the sidewalk. He waited until the hunter had disappeared round a corner then he followed, keeping well behind, but always with Martin in his sights. No way was he going to let this opportunity slip through his fingers. To be there when a real vampire was actually trapped and captured would put Billy's face on the front page of every publication in the US, if not the world. He wanted that fame — and the fortune that would undoubtedly follow.

And no skinny guy with an attitude is going to stop me — no way, Jose!

* * * *

Lonnie, the Xtasy Club owner, looked over the accounting printouts Chris had given him and shook his head. "You do good work, kid," he said. "I can't persuade you to stay? I'll make it worth your while."

Chris smiled at his soon to be ex-boss. "No thanks, Lonnie, but I do appreciate it. You've all been very nice to me here. It's just that I have a new job offer, and I have my folks' accounts to take care of, too."

"Sure, sure." Lonnie handed him an envelope. "A little something extra for you in there. You find anyone interested in taking your place?"

"'Fraid not, but if I hear of anyone looking for work, I'll give them your phone number."

Lonnie grunted then looked through the office window. "That big guy yours?" Lonnie nodded in the direction of the bar where Carlos was waiting for Chris.

Chris chuckled. "I like to think he is."

"Looks like he can take care of himself all right. Joe was tellin' me he beat the shit outta some morons in the alley."

"Yes," Chris said proudly. "Actually that's how we first met."

"Yeah, well tell him to watch his back. The punks might've been a bunch of cowards, with shit for brains, but he put their noses outta joint and made them look stupider than they already are. So they might just want to get even with you and your boyfriend."

"Don't worry, I've got my car parked outside." Chris rattled his car keys. "No more walking up the alley."

"Okay, kid." Lonnie held out his hand. "Take it easy, and come by any time. Drinks are on the house."

"Thanks, Lonnie." Chris shook the man's hand then walked quickly over to where Carlos stood by the bar having a glass of wine. He reached up to kiss Carlos on the cheek, at the same time rubbing his hand over the tall man's butt.

Carlos smiled at him. "Do I understand from that you might be ready to go?"

"More than ready. I can't wait to get you home."

Carlos threw back the last of his wine. "Then, as they say in American movies, let's blow this joint."

Chris giggled. "The whole joint?"

Laughing together, their arms about each other, they headed for the exit.

* * * *

Martin stood for a few moments looking up at the lighted window of Chris' apartment then he slipped into the shadows to prepare himself for the kill. He had weighed the options of waiting for a daytime strike, but the chance that had now presented itself was too good to ignore. The vampire was with his mortal lover. No doubt he would be distracted enough to let his senses be more attuned to carnal desire than to his own safety. But just in case…

From the leather bag he carried, he removed a small aerosol vial and sprayed his face and hands with a fine mist. This secret herbal mixture would mask his human scent and allow him to get close without being detected, as long as he stayed hidden from the vampire's sight. He pulled a length of silver chain from his bag, looping it loosely and weighing it carefully in his hand before placing it carefully into his coat pocket.

He moved forward and stared up at the long balcony. *An easy climb*, he thought, gripping the limbs of the vines that grew in profusion, covering the apartment building's walls. He scaled the wall and peered through the balcony railing. The vampire and his friend were standing at the far end wrapped in each other's arms.

Perfect. He pulled his knife from the scabbard inside his coat. He knew the vampire couldn't scent him. He could get as close as he wanted, gaining the advantage of a surprise strike.

The sound of rustling behind him made him freeze. *Another one? No. It's that fool, Billy Richards, climbing up onto the balcony. Damn him to hell! He would alert the vampire – the vampire would scent him.* Even as Martin's mind closed around that fact, Carlos turned, and Martin knew the vampire's senses were alive to everything that surrounded him, to everything that was a danger to him. A low growl erupted from the vampire's throat. Behind him, Martin heard Billy squeak with fear.

The fool, he'll get us both killed! It was now or never. Martin launched himself forward, his knife raised to strike. He felt his wrist grabbed in a bone snapping grip. His scream of agony was cut off as the vampire's hand encircled his throat and squeezed, hard.

Then a shout of shocked surprise resounded in Martin's ears. "Carlos! Oh, Jesus — "

Immediately, the grip on Martin's throat relaxed, and he was thrown backwards across the balcony.

"Christopher, get inside, now!"

Martin looked up as the tall vampire turned away from him and spoke rapidly to the kid from the Xtasy Club.

"Get inside now, *please*," the vampire repeated, and Martin seized his advantage. Springing to his feet, he brought his silver knife down in a sweeping arc, driving it with all his strength between the vampire's shoulder blades.

No sound escaped the vampire's lips, but his body stiffened under the impact of Martin's blow. As Martin held on to the knife's hilt with both hands, driving it deeper, Carlos fell to his knees, and a long low moan of pain mingled with despair was wrenched from him. Martin pulled the chain from his pocket and wound it around Carlos' neck. Martin opened his mouth to yell in victory, to say the words of triumph handed down through the ages, from vampire hunter to vampire hunter — the words that would seal the vampire's fate and turn him to dust.

"*Serrato, serranus — *"

He got no further, for a sudden violent and excruciating pain erupted on the side of his head. He staggered back, releasing his hold on the knife's hilt and stared through a red mist at the cause of his agony. The young guy from the club was holding a brick in his hand, a brick he swung a second time, this time whacking Martin on his jaw. Martin screamed with pain and rage, reaching for help from Billy who stood stock still, his eyes wide with terror at the scene before him. Then a thin wail of hysteria rose from Billy's slack mouth as Carlos staggered to his feet, wrenched the chain from around his neck and threw it away.

"You didn't finish him," Billy screamed, turning to run. Martin grabbed him, and despite the debilitating pain in his head that threatened to bring him to his knees, he threw Billy into Carlos' path. Billy's wail of terror increased in volume. He was lifted off the ground as if he weighed nothing at all then pitched over the balcony rail to land with a sickening thud on the concrete path.

Carlos advanced on Martin, but the hunter had just enough strength to lift himself over the balcony and drop onto the soft grass below. Without waiting to determine Billy's fate, he ran across the apartment grounds and disappeared into the darkness.

Chris stared with horror at Carlos' blood-drenched shirt, at the black-hilted knife that protruded from his lover's back and fought back the nausea that rose in his throat. He took Carlos' arm and led him back inside the apartment.

"I...I'll call 9-1-1," he stammered, wondering how on earth Carlos was able to stay upright. "I don't dare pull the knife out. You might bleed to death. The paramedics will know what to do."

"No, there's no need to call them," Carlos muttered, his ragged voice reflecting his agony. "I have already called for help."

"Huh?" Chris gazed at his pain-filled face without understanding. Was the trauma of the attack making him hallucinate? He hadn't called anyone—

A loud knocking at the door startled him. *Who the...?*

"Who's there?" he yelled.

"Marcus and Roger. May we enter?"

"Oh, thank God," Chris exclaimed, running to the door. He swung it open. "Come in quick. Carlos has been hurt—*stabbed*. Two guys came out of nowhere. I was just going to call 9-1-1."

"That won't be necessary," Marcus told him then turned to Carlos and said, "Brace yourself, my friend."

Carlos nodded. "Do it, quickly."

Marcus gripped the knife hilt, and with one swift motion, he pulled the blade free. He handed the knife to Roger then pulled Carlos' shirt off and threw it to one side. Chris gasped, feeling sick at the sight of the blood that poured from the wound.

Marcus covered the gash with his hand. "Roger, take Chris into the bedroom. What I must do is not for his eyes."

Roger put down the knife on the coffee table and took Chris' arm. "Come on. He'll yell when it's over."

"When what's over?" Chris tried unsuccessfully to free his arm from Roger's powerful grip. "What's he going to do?"

"Now, Roger," Marcus snapped.

Chris was unable to resist as Roger hustled him across the room and into the bedroom then shut the door firmly behind them.

* * * *

"Lie down," Marcus said, helping Carlos to lie prone on the rug. He straddled Carlos' thighs, his hand still pressed firmly to the wound, staunching the flow of blood. "My blood will negate the poison from the silver. Be very still."

He bit into his left wrist, then removing his hand from the wound, he squeezed his blood into the gaping gash on Carlos' back. Fortunately, the knife had missed Carlos' spine. The silver would have done more damage to his nervous system had it penetrated there. Marcus watched as the infection around the wound faded, and the torn flesh began to knit. He spat onto his fingers and rubbed his saliva over the livid scar until it too faded away.

"Drink now," Marcus murmured, holding out his wrist to Carlos as he sat up. "I have fed this evening so you will not weaken me. Then we must do something about your shirt."

After drinking the offered blood, Carlos raised his head from Marcus' wrist and smiled gratefully at his friend. "Thank you." He kissed Marcus tenderly. "I let my guard down tonight. I was foolish—"

"You are in love, Carlos." Marcus stroked his friend's face gently. "You put your lover's safety before your own, as was proper."

Carlos grimaced. "And again, I have brought danger into his life."

Marcus nodded. He picked up the knife from the coffee table and slipped it into his jacket's inside pocket.

"I'm afraid that goes with the territory," he said with a sad smile.

* * * *

Chris glared at his new friend. "What's going on, Roger?" he asked, rubbing his arm where Roger had gripped it hard. "Why aren't we calling the paramedics?"

"Uh, that could be awkward." For once, Roger seemed lost for words.

"Why awkward? Carlos needs medical attention— and right away!"

"That's what Marcus is giving him. Uh, medical attention."

"Marcus is a doctor?"

"Not exactly."

"Well, *what* exactly? Roger, this is not the time for fucking around." Chris marched towards the door. "You saw that wound. It needs stitches and antibiotics. He needs a doctor!"

Roger stepped in front of the door as Chris tried to open it.

"What are you doing?" Chris yelled. "Let me outta here!"

"Please, Chris." Roger didn't move away. "I can't let you in there 'til Marcus says I can."

Chris tried to push Roger out of the way. He gaped at Roger in amazement when he couldn't budge him one inch. They were roughly the same height and build, but Roger seemed to be immensely strong. Chris pushed harder.

"Chris, don't. Just wait a few minutes. It'll be all right, you'll see."

"How come you're so damned strong?" Chris panted. "Lemme pass, you son-of-a—"

"Roger," Marcus called out, "You may bring Christopher in here now."

"Sorry," Roger mumbled, before he moved aside and opened the door.

Chris rushed into the living room and stopped short, unable to believe his eyes. Carlos, shirtless, and looking fit and healthy, smiled at him. Chris hurried into his arms.

"Oh, thank God," he murmured, his lips trembling on Carlos' neck. "You're all right. It looked so much worse than it obviously was."

"Yes." Carlos kissed Chris' forehead. "Some quick action from Marcus saved me a trip to the hospital."

"Amazing." Chris looked at Marcus. "What was it you didn't want me to see?"

"Oh, just some laying on of hands," Marcus said quietly. "Some people get squeamish watching it, so it's best done in private."

"You mean like *faith* healing?" Chris slipped from Carlos' arms and walked behind him. He touched Carlos' back. "There's no sign of a scar anywhere. That's impossible. A knife went in here, *deep*. Now there's no scar. How can that be?" Chris looked from one man to the other, waiting for an answer. None came.

Roger, coughing quietly into his hand, broke the silence. "Good thing though is that Carlos is okay," he said, grinning.

Chris frowned at him. "And you. You seemed to have way more strength than you should. We're almost the same build, but you—"

He broke off mid-sentence, not knowing what he was going to say next. He looked at Carlos. "Why aren't you wearing your shirt?"

Carlos smiled at him. "Don't you remember? You took it off me, just before Marcus and Roger arrived." Carlos picked up his shirt , now unmarked by bloodstains, and slipped it on.

"Yeah, sorry to interrupt," Roger said, chuckling. "We were in the neighbourhood and thought we'd stop by. See if you guys wanted to go out for a drink."

"But we can see you were otherwise occupied." Marcus winked at Chris. "So we won't stay. Come along, Roger."

"No, wait…" Chris felt confused. He couldn't remember them arriving, yet here they were, and he hadn't even offered them a drink. He smiled weakly. "Some host, I am. Can I get you something? I have some home-grown wine."

"No, thank you." Marcus put his arm around Roger's shoulders and steered him towards the door. "We'll leave you to enjoy one another's company."

"We'll see you tomorrow night. Our place," Roger said, waving goodnight. "Later!"

"Right, later." Chris watched them leave, returning Roger's little wave and smile. He looked at Carlos, slightly puzzled. "I feel like I've just missed something..."

Carlos pulled him into his arms and kissed him soundly. Marcus had averted what could possibly have been an awkward confrontation. Chris now had no memory of the hunter's attack.

"Why don't we resume what we were doing," Carlos murmured. "I think that's what you're missing. I'll just close the window. It's getting a little chilly, don't you think?"

Chris grinned. "For someone as hot-blooded as you, you sure feel the cold a lot."

"It's my Spanish blood." Carlos stepped out onto the balcony and looked down at the patio area below. There was no sign of the man he'd thrown over the railing earlier. He must have recovered enough to make a getaway. Carlos surveyed the dark grounds surrounding the apartment complex through narrowed eyes. His extrasensory vampire sight could discern no suspicious movement around them, only the normal comings and goings of the other residents. Satisfied there would be no further attacks this evening, he stepped back inside, then closed and locked the window.

"Come over here." Chris opened his arms. "Let me take that shirt off you again."

Smiling, Carlos complied, relief flooding over him now that he knew the danger had passed. As he enfolded Chris in his embrace, he vowed he would never be so lax as to let the hunter anywhere near them again.

Chapter Twelve

Frank swore with irritation at the sound of the insistent banging on his door. "Who the fuck—?" *It better not be Billy with that moron he's picked up with,* he thought darkly, marching over to the door. He swung it open and gaped at the man who pushed past him, staggered over to the couch and fell onto it with a groan.

"Billy, what the hell happened to you?" He stared at his friend who looked like he'd been in a wreck. His T-shirt was ripped, his forehead bloody, his arms covered in welts and bruises.

"The vampire you said doesn't exist threw me off a balcony, that's what happened to me," Billy seethed. "That stupid son-of-a-bitch, so-called vampire hunter blew it. He couldn't kill him. He got up, even after Martin had stabbed him in the back and wrapped a chain round his neck."

Frank poured a shot of Jack Daniel's then handed it to Billy. "He stabbed him in the back, and the vamp — the *guy* got up?"

Billy threw back the entire shot and licked his lips. "That kid from the Xtasy club slammed Martin on the head with a brick."

"No shit."

"Martin ran, leaving me there with that monster." Billy started to cry. "I thought I was dead, Frank. I thought he'd tear out my throat."

"But instead he tossed you over the balcony. Lucky break, I'd say."

"This isn't funny, Frank." Billy swiped at the tears spilling from his eyes. "I coulda been killed."

"Because you got yourself mixed up with that nutcase who thinks he's a vampire hunter," Frank sneered. "Maybe you'll listen to me now, Billy. The guy's a homicidal maniac, and if you don't keep away from him, you'll go down with him."

"But the guy he's stalking is a vampire, Frank."

"Oh, for fuck's sake, Billy!"

"I'm telling you he is. If you'd seen him tonight — blood pouring from him and still able to pick me up like I weighed nothin' at all."

"Yeah, well maybe after losing all that blood, the fucker's dead and you don't have to worry about any of this again. Count yourself lucky you got away with bruises and not a broken neck." Frank filled Billy's outstretched glass with another shot. "Forget about vampires and vampire hunters, Billy."

Billy threw back the second shot and closed his eyes. His dirty cheeks were streaked with tear trails. "Mind if I stay over tonight, Frank? I can lay here on the couch, if that's okay."

Frank sighed and stared at his buddy for a moment or two. He felt a strange twinge of compassion. *The stupid s.o.b. looks like shit*, he thought. *Maybe he's learned his lesson and will stick to robbing old ladies instead of chasing imaginary vampires.*

"Sure, I guess. Make yourself to home—but just for tonight, okay?"

"Thanks, Frank," Billy murmured and fell asleep.

* * * *

Martin, holding an ice pack to his swollen face, stared angrily at his reflection in the mirror. Twice now he had failed—thwarted again by the kid from the club. More than he hated vampires, he now hated that kid. He was going to make him suffer—big time. Time he knew just what he was dealing with. Time to burst his pretty balloon and tell him the party's over.

"Because, *Christopher*," Martin said aloud, "the man you're so in love with is a vampire. And before I'm finished with you, you'll believe it, just in time to see him crumble to dust in front of your stupid, infatuated eyes."

And Billy. The idiot responsible for this evening's disaster. If he hadn't followed Martin, hadn't been there, the vampire wouldn't have been alerted to his presence, wouldn't have had his senses on fire with the imminent danger surrounding him. Martin could have been in control, struck the vampire down quickly, and it would have been over before Chris had even realised what was going on.

He'd like to take Billy and beat him within an inch of his life. Martin glared at his livid expression, breathing hard, trying to control his rage. He couldn't afford to let his emotions get in the way of what he still had to do. He needed a clear head, a calm mind, and he was going to have to be much more careful next time. The vampire was strong—stronger than any he had encountered before. Yet Martin was loath to call for help. He could contact Vince, his old partner— someone to act as a decoy then a back up once they had the vampire cornered. But he was in no frame of mind to split the bounty he'd earn on a vampire kill with Vince. He figured the best way to get to the vampire was still through Chris. He just had to get the kid alone—and the best time for that was during the day. His vampire buddy wouldn't be around then— and, Martin thought ruefully, he'd make damned sure the kid didn't have access to hot coffee or bricks!

Still scowling, he examined the damage Chris had done to his face. It would be a couple of days before the swelling was gone, and he'd feel like going on the hunt again. Muttering to himself, he paced the small rented room. He paused to pull a flask containing whisky from his travelling bag and splashed a sizeable amount into a plastic glass.

Two or three of these might ease the pain.

Slumping onto the room's narrow bed and trying to ignore the throbbing pain in his head, he began to devise a new plan.

* * * *

Carlos raised an eyebrow as Roger entered the living room carrying a big bowl of potato chips and another containing some kind of dip.

"Smells awful, huh?" Roger grinned at him. "Garlic. Can't believe I used to love this kind of thing. Chris will think it's yummy though."

"Ugh, garlic breath," Carlos said, chuckling. "You're ruining my plans for some goodnight kissing."

"Eh, you can handle it," Roger told him. He glanced at his watch. "Almost eight, he should be arriving any minute now."

Carlos nodded. "I sense him approaching the driveway. Shall I let him in, or did you want to act the perfect host?"

"Let Marcus do it. He enjoys welcoming new guests to his home." He looked across the room to where Micah and Joseph sat by the fireplace, their arms about one another. "Just look at those two, will you? Together for over a year and they still act like lovesick teens."

"They've been through a lot of hard times in that year," Carlos said quietly. "Marcus told me of their encounter with Darius."

"Yeah." Roger looked over again at his friends. "Micah really had an initiation by fire at the hands of that bastard, Darius. Funny how we never hear anything of the Dark Forces since he was executed."

"I understand the new leaders believe in keeping a low profile." Carlos followed Roger's gaze. "Joseph and Micah truly deserve the happiness they have found together."

"Just as you deserve happiness with Chris." Roger absently bit into a potato chip then gagged. "Yuck! Did I mention I used to like this stuff?"

Carlos laughed. "You did and garlic dip."

Roger shuddered. "So, when do you plan on telling him?"

"I don't know." Carlos poured himself a glass of wine. "I know I must, sooner rather than later, but I fear it might just be too much for him to comprehend."

Roger's eyes twinkled with mischief. "I could drop a few more of those pointed remarks that Marcus loves so much. Chris might just start to put two and two together."

"Roger, imagine how he would feel if he suddenly realised he was sitting in a room full of vampires." Carlos shook his head. "Please don't try to help me here."

"I shall be the soul of tact and discretion." Roger giggled and kissed Carlos on the cheek. "Now, I can hear him talking to Marcus. Off you go and give him a big sloppy kiss — before he gets garlic breath!"

* * * *

The evening went smoothly enough. Chris seemed at ease in everyone's company and Carlos found himself relaxing as they sat together on the couch watching the movie. Chris rested his head on Carlos' shoulder and surreptitiously slipped his hand inside Carlos' shirt to tease his nipples. Chris found himself thinking that even the studly Hugh Jackman had a lot of competition in the looks department right there in the room.

Marcus, curled up with Roger in one of the large armchairs, groaned a few times during the movie, but otherwise was quiet, while Micah and Joseph seemed more interested in one another than in the movie.

"Where on earth did the notion that a werewolf could kill a vampire come from?" Marcus demanded when the movie had finished and Roger had turned some of the lights back on.

"From the screenwriter's imagination I should think," Carlos said quickly.

"Oh, of course." Marcus had caught the warning in Carlos' voice.

Roger chuckled and punched Marcus lightly on the arm. "A slip of the tongue?"

"*Touché*, Roger."

"Yeah, I wondered about that bit," Chris said, getting everyone's attention. "I'd never heard that before. And wouldn't Bram Stoker be surprised to learn that Van Helsing was a werewolf."

"A bit of a stretch," Roger agreed. "And Dracula seemed a bit wimpy to me. I mean, a real vampire could never be put down quite as easy."

Chris laughed lightly. "A *real* vampire?"

"Roger," Marcus interrupted. "Why don't you pour everyone a glass of wine, and let's talk about something else."

"Like what?" Roger asked ,walking over to the bar for a bottle of wine.

"For instance, Christopher's new position in Carlos' export company."

"Well, I haven't really started that yet," Chris said. "But I'm really looking forward to it." He smiled shyly. "Knowing the boss as well as I do is a definite perk."

"And you'll be working quite closely with Joseph." Carlos hugged Chris to him. "Joseph takes care of my investment portfolio," he added by way of explanation, "so you and he will confer from time to time on acquisitions and the like."

"Sounds exciting." Chris smiled across at Joseph then at Micah. "What do you do, Micah?"

Micah's smile was a tad rueful. "I used to manage a bookstore, but I got fired for running off to Paris with Joseph, so I'm kind of looking for something."

"Half-heartedly looking," Roger interjected, chuckling. "For almost a year."

Chris got the idea neither of these two young men had to work for a living — their lovers were obviously very wealthy. He wasn't sure how he felt about that. Carlos was wealthy too, but the idea of being kept by him was not something Chris could entertain. Not that it meant he thought less of Micah and Roger because of it.

He was suddenly aware that all the men were looking at him as though they knew exactly what was going through his mind. Damn. Roger had even said he was clairvoyant. What if he hadn't been joking?

"Well," he said weakly, "jobs aren't that easy to find these days. I'm very lucky Carlos offered me this great job."

"Let's drink to that," Roger said cheerfully, filling Chris' wine glass. "To Chris' new job and, may I be the first to say it, to his new life with Carlos."

Chris blushed and smiled happily at the toast. A life with Carlos. He couldn't ask for anything more wonderful than that.

* * * *

"I hope you weren't embarrassed by Roger's toast to our future together," Carlos remarked as Chris drove them to his apartment.

"I liked it," Chris said at once. "I hope you did, too."

"I very much like the idea of you and I spending the rest of our lives together, Christopher." Carlos hesitated, then said, "Of course there will have to be some adjustments made. I mean, my home is not here in LA."

"Right. I understand." Chris didn't like the idea of Carlos being away for long periods of time, but surely they could work something out. "And I do have my parents' business accounting to attend to."

"Have you ever been to Madrid, Christopher?"

"Never. The only foreign travel I've done is to France. My parents took me there five years ago. We did a tour of the vineyards in Southern France."

"Is your passport still valid?"

"Oh, yeah. Good for another five years or so."

"Good. I may have to ask that you accompany me at short notice, so a valid passport is a must."

"Wow. You and me in Madrid. Could life get any sweeter?"

Carlos smiled and squeezed Chris' thigh then ran his hand up to Chris' crotch. "I can think of infinite ways my life can be made sweeter — just by being with you." He leant over and nuzzled Chris' neck.

Chris groaned. "Oh, man. Wait 'til I park this thing, will you? I'd hate like hell to ruin what's coming by wrecking the car." He swung the car into the apartment parking lot, cut the engine then launched himself into Carlos' arms. "You drive me wild," he muttered before taking his lover's lips with his own.

"This is nice," Carlos said when they came up for air, "but there's more room in your apartment."

"True." Chris give him a quick peck on the lips. "Let's go."

Hand in hand, they ran up the steps to Chris' front door then stopped short as they caught sight of a sheet of paper pinned to the door.

"What the hell?" Chris tore it free and stared at the two words printed on the paper. *Vampire Bait.* His eyes met Carlos' dark-green gaze. "That crazy man from the club must have put this here. How did he know where I lived?" He balled the paper in his fist and threw it to one side in disgust.

"Let's go inside," Carlos said quietly.

"Shit." Chris unlocked the door. "I don't like the idea of him snooping around here. That guy gave me the creeps."

Carlos took his arm. "Wait while I check inside."

But Chris entered the apartment alongside Carlos. "I'm not having you walk into some trap alone." He flicked on the light and locked the door behind him. The apartment gave no sign of having been entered or anything touched in his absence.

"What the hell is his fixation with vampires, anyway? The guy must be totally insane."

Carlos checked out the bedroom then came back into the living room and gazed at Chris for a long moment in silence. Roger's words echoed in his mind. *When are you going to tell him?* He hadn't wanted it to be like this, but the vampire hunter was a very real and present danger and had now made it plain that Christopher was no longer safe.

"Christopher…" The words he had to say seemed unwilling to be forced from his lips. "The man who confronted you in the club is a vampire hunter, and he is hunting — me."

"What?" The expression on Chris' face changed from one of incredulity to a slow smile as he imagined Carlos was joking. "Okay, that's funny, but the fact he was here isn't too cool. Should I call the cops and report it, do you think?"

Carlos took one step nearer. "Listen to me, Christopher. What I am telling you is the truth. Two nights ago, the man attacked me right here on your balcony. Had it not been for your quick action of hitting him with a brick, he might have succeeded in killing me."

Chris closed his eyes, shook his head then opened his eyes and stared at Carlos. "Okay, it's really you telling me this. I'm not hallucinating, but what you just said makes no sense whatsoever. There was a guy on the balcony attacking you, and I hit him — with a brick. How come I have absolutely no memory of that?" He grinned suddenly. "You're still joking, right? Is this a little role playing thing you want to get into? You want to wrestle or something?" Chris laughed. "I can be up for that."

"I am not joking, Christopher. All of what I have just said is the truth. The vampire hunter was here."

"*Carlos…*"

"Remember when Marcus and Roger arrived unexpectedly the other night?"

"Yes."

"They came because I called to them for help."

"Oh, so they're vampires, too?"

"Yes."

"Oh, for Pete's sake! Carlos, why are you doing this?"

Carlos sighed, his eyes filled with concern. "Believe me, I didn't want to have to tell you like this. I've never been sure of how I would tell you what I am. There are ways of course that make the telling easier for me—and for you hearing it, less of a shock. I could put you in my thrall and ease the pain that usually follows the revelation, but there is always the fear that follows, regardless of how it's done. Eventually, in the cold light of day, you would come to realise the truth."

Chris continued to stare at him, disbelief clouding his eyes. "This just doesn't make any sense. Are you trying to break up with me or something? If you are, there are less crazy ways to do it."

"I am not trying to break up with you." Carlos touched Chris' face gently. "Nothing could be further from my mind, but in a moment, when you believe what I'm saying to be the truth, you may not want me in your life anymore."

"So, you're sticking with your story—about being a vampire, I mean."

"Yes, I'm afraid I am."

"Prove it."

"What?"

"Prove it. Prove to me that you're a vampire. Turn into a bat or fly around the room — do *something*."

"I can't turn into a bat."

"I knew it."

"And flying around this small room might be somewhat ungainly."

"Carlos." Chris heaved a sigh of relief mixed with impatience. He walked into Carlos' arms and held him tight. "You are no more a vampire than I am. I don't know why you're playing this silly joke, but I'm over it so let's drop it and make love."

Carlos cupped Chris' face between his hands and kissed him tenderly. "I could say, 'Look into my eyes, and all will be revealed'."

Chris giggled. "That old corny Dracula routine. *Look into my eyes*," he intoned, gazing up at Carlos. "Oh, my God…"

He was in the alleyway. The thugs pressed around him and Carlos. He heard a gunshot. Heard himself scream, "No!" Saw Carlos stagger back. He had been hit. Oh Jesus, his face, his teeth. Another shot — pain. I've been shot. Carlos…with me…giving me his blood…drinking his blood —

Chris, his face ashen with shock, wrenched himself from Carlos' embrace. "It-it's true. You are what you said. Oh my God. Oh my *God — No*." He backed up several steps until he hit the wall.

"Please don't be afraid of me, Christopher. You are in no danger from me."

"No? I'd rather take my chances with that creepy guy. A cup of coffee in the face and it was over, but you…?" A sudden realisation hit him. "And tonight, watching that movie with Marcus and Roger and...and — they're *all* vampires?" His voice held a slight edge of hysteria. "Oh, my God!"

"Christopher." Carlos reached for Chris and drew him into his arms. Chris whimpered, suddenly powerless to resist. His body stiffened in the vampire's embrace. He closed his eyes, certain now that his throat was about to be ripped open.

"Carlos, please. Don't..."

"Christopher, listen to me. I will not harm you. I love you. I am not some soulless creature of the night, desiring only your blood." Carlos tilted Chris' head back. His heart twisted with grief at the look of fear on the young man's face. *Surely there must have been a better way for him to know*, he thought. "Christopher," he murmured, his voice soft and seductive. "I mean what I say. I love you, and I will never hurt you. Look at me, *querido*. Do you believe me?"

Trembling, Chris gazed up into gaze into the depths of Carlos' golden brown eyes. *Yes, so beautiful*, Carlos heard Chris think, *but belonging to someone I believed I was going to love for the rest of my life, someone I'm now scared to death of, someone I have to get away from.*

"I...I can't."

Carlos released him and stepped back, his expression one of total sadness. "Then I am sorry. Christopher, I must leave you. And I must take with me all the memories you have of what we shared, memories only I can now cherish for all eternity."

Gently, he brushed Chris' lips with the softest of kisses then tilted Chris' face until their eyes met and held.

"Goodbye, *querido*," he whispered, then like a silent shadow caught in a ray of light, he was gone.

Chapter Thirteen

"Huh?" Chris looked around his apartment, just for a moment thinking he'd heard someone telling him goodbye. "Must be hearing things," he muttered, fishing his cell phone out of his pocket to answer its strident tones. "Hello?"

"Hi, Chris, how's it goin'?"

"Hey, Joey. Pretty good."

"Another heavy date with you-know-who?"

"If I knew who 'you-know-who' was, I might be able to answer that dumb question. I've been home all night by myself."

"No Carlos tonight?"

"Who?"

"*Carlos*. Your main man, your Spanish *caballero* in shining armour."

"Joey, I don't know what you're talking about. There's no one called Carlos in my life."

"Oh, shit, I'm sorry. I didn't realise you two had split up."

"Joey, quit fucking with me."

"I'm sorry. It's okay. I mean, it'll *be* okay. Want some company?"

"No, it's late. I'm going to bed—but thanks."

"That's what friends are for. So, you wanna take in a movie tomorrow night?"

"Sounds good. I'll call you tomorrow."

"Okay—and Chris, take it easy."

"Will do. Ciao."

"Ciao."

Chris closed his phone, shaking his head. What the hell was Joey talking about? He must have gotten him mixed up with one of his other friends. What an airhead.

* * * *

Joey stared at the phone in his hand for a moment or two before closing it and putting it down on the kitchen counter.

Poor Chris, he'd had such high hopes for a relationship with Carlos. Wonder what happened? Must have been bad 'cause Chris is in total denial. Carlos…who? Jeez, but life was a bitch sometimes. Chris is such a cool guy, so nice, and Carlos had sounded just the perfect guy for him. Sweet and caring, Chris had said.

"Wish I could find someone sweet and caring," he said aloud. "But then, he'd probably go the way of all hot flesh—just like Carlos."

Joey vowed he would not mention the name 'Carlos' again until Chris was ready to talk about him and what had happened.

* * * *

Carlos hovered over Chris' apartment building, his dark clothing making him invisible against the moonless sky. Even though he was no longer to be a part of Chris' life, he would not abandon him until he was absolutely certain Martin Kellogg was no longer a danger to him. His eyes swept the grounds, the nearby trees, the streets beyond. All seemed quiet and normal for—he glanced at his watch—a few minutes after midnight. After one long circular flight over the area, he felt satisfied all would be well this evening. He flew higher then headed in the direction of Hollywood Hills.

Marcus and Roger were standing on the terrace when he alighted there a few minutes later. There was no need to tell them what had occurred—they already knew. Roger embraced him, hugging him tightly to his body.

"I'm sorry, big guy," he murmured. "I know how much Chris meant to you, how much he still means to you."

Carlos patted Roger on the back then stepped away from his embrace. "I don't think I will ever forget the look of abject terror on his face when he finally realised what I am." He looked keenly at Roger. "Were you not terrified when Marcus revealed himself to you?"

"Of course, I was. I almost peed my pants. I kept waiting for him to chew on my neck." Roger smiled, remembering. "Then he kissed me."

"That's all it took?"

"Well, he cheated a little." A quiet cough behind him made him laugh. "Well, you did Marcus. You used that special thing you have that makes you irresistible."

"You mean he put you in his thrall." Carlos sighed heavily. "Something I could have done of course."

"Not in my thrall," Marcus said. "Roger was aware of everything that was happening. I did not coerce him with my powers."

"Then what?" Carlos looked confused. "What else could I have done?"

"It's in his kiss," Roger said, smiling up at his lover. "Unfortunately, not all vampires have it. Something in his saliva blurs the senses, calms and arouses at the same time. At least, that's how it was for me. I was scared, but I wanted him more than I had ever wanted anyone in my life."

Carlos looked at them both and shook his head slowly. "I told him I loved him, that I would never hurt him, and still I could not quell his fear of me."

"Mortals have an inherent fear of us, Carlos." Marcus took him by the arm and led him inside. "What they know of us they have read in books and seen in movies — like the one we watched earlier. We are evil monsters, bent on sucking all human blood and turning them into mindless slaves to satisfy our lust."

"Whereas, we're only scary 'til you get to know us," Roger quipped.

Marcus poured Carlos a glass of wine. "You are worried that the hunter may still be a danger to Christopher."

"Yes. When we arrived at his apartment there was a note on his door. Two words. *Vampire Bait.*"

"That son-of-a-bitch," Roger muttered.

"I have to track him," Carlos said grimly. "I have to hunt him down before he can harm Christopher — or any one of our friends."

Marcus nodded. "All our friends in LA have been alerted to the fact he is out there. Joseph has contacted the Vampire Council for more information on the man. Who he works for, his contacts, etc. He should have the information soon. From what you have said, it sounds like Kellogg works alone."

"There was another man with him, the one I threw over the balcony, but he seemed to be in the way, not Kellogg's partner. However, now when I think about it, he did look familiar." He paused. "Of course, now I remember. He was one of the thugs in the alley — probably the one who reported seeing a vampire."

"And Kellogg would have contacted him," Marcus said, "being one of the few who would have believed the story."

"At any rate, he is unimportant. After seeing how little Kellogg thought of him, throwing him at me so he could escape, I doubt if the man will be willing to be associated with Kellogg again."

* * * *

Chris woke the following morning and, for the first time in a while, felt at a loss for something to do. Now that the exams were over, and hopefully the results would be sent to him in a few days, he supposed he should go home and set up the office space his father had set aside for him. Pulling on his sweats, he thought of the day ahead. After coffee and a bagel from the corner coffee shop, he'd go work out for a while. Oh, and Joey had mentioned a movie for later. Maybe tomorrow, he'd drive up to Santa Barbara so he and his dad could get started on the office.

Funny, but he couldn't quite shake the impression that there was something else he should be thinking of — or was it *someone* else? That was nuts, for sure. There wasn't a someone in his life at present. So why did he have this haunting feeling that something, someone, had gone from his life? Sighing, he pulled on his trainers, grabbed a few dollars from his jeans' pocket and headed for the door.

Locking up, he noticed a crumpled ball of paper lying on the ground near his door. He was just about to kick it out of the way when he noticed there were some printed words on it. He picked the ball of paper up and smoothed it out.

"Vampire bait," he muttered. "What the hell does that mean?"

"It means you, *Christopher*."

The voice coming from right behind him made him jump and whirl round. He stared in shock at the man who had accosted him in the club. From his bruised and swollen face, it looked like he'd been in a fight.

"You-you're the guy from the club. What are you doing here?"

"You and I have something in common." Martin Kellogg leered at Chris. "Shall we go inside and talk?"

"No, we shall not." Chris started to walk away. "You and I have nothing in common, Mister — especially your fixation with vampires. Now beat it before I call the cops."

Martin grabbed Chris' arm and spun him against the wall. "Listen to me," he hissed, keeping a grip on Chris' arm. "Your tall friend is a vampire, and you will show me where he rests."

"Fuck off, you moron!" Chris yelled into Martin's face and brought his knee up into the man's crotch. Gagging and cursing, Martin doubled over, releasing Chris who sprinted down the stairs, out onto the street almost knocking over a man jogging past the building.

"Hey, watch out!" the jogger yelled.

"Sorry," Chris panted. "Some asshole attacked me outside my apartment."

The jogger peered at Chris. "You look a bit shaken up. There's a highway patrol car parked at the corner. Let's go tell the officer."

The police officer must have seen Chris barrelling out onto the street. His car cruised up to where Chris and the jogger were standing.

"What's going on guys?"

The jogger said, "He was attacked outside his apartment."

The police officer heaved himself out of the car. Chris felt like a midget next to him. The man must have weighed close to three hundred pounds and sported a badge that read 'Officer Zimbowskie'.

"Let's go take a look."

Chris started to lead the way back to his apartment, but the cop stopped him at the bottom of the steps and pulled out his gun. "Can't be too careful," he muttered, climbing the steps with a ponderous tread. Chris followed close behind, the jogger behind him.

"Careful when you get to the top," Chris said. 'There's a bit of a blind corner there."

"Got it covered," Zimbowskie wheezed, the climb having taken its toll on his overweight frame. "Nope, nobody here."

Chris hadn't really expected the man to be still lurking about, but the crumpled sheet of paper he'd found earlier was there where he'd dropped it.

"He left this," Chris said, picking it up and handing it over to Zimbowskie who holstered his gun and peered at the paper.

"Vampire bait?"

"He came to the club I used to work in a few nights ago and started babbling about vampires. The guy is obviously insane."

"There's a lot of them around, son. Well, looks like he's taken off. I'll cruise around the neighbourhood and make sure he's gone. You wanna file a report?"

Chris hesitated, then said, "No, that's all right. I'm going out of town for a few days anyway. Maybe he'll find someone else to pester in the meantime."

"Okay, if you're sure. I'll alert the officer who relieves me, and he'll keep an eye open for any strange guys — or vampires — hanging around." Zimbowskie chuckled at his joke, then he and the jogger turned to leave. Chris followed them down the steps then headed for his original destination. He really needed that coffee now!

* * * *

Joey called Chris later that day. "Still on for the movies?"

"Yeah, just make sure it's not about vampires."

"I thought you liked vampire movies," Joey chuckled.

"I used to, but I've got this creep stalking me, telling me he's a vampire hunter and I have to show him where they *rest*."

"Shut up! Where'd he come from?"

"Who knows. He was outside my apartment this morning, leaving a note that said I was vampire bait."

"Chris…" Joey's voice deepened with concern. "This is not good. You'd better stay over at my place tonight."

"I might just take you up on that. The guy kinda creeped me out. Anyway, I'll pick you up about six, okay?"

"Okay. And bring your toothbrush."

* * * *

Frowning, Joey closed his cell phone. *Poor Chris*, he thought. *He just can't catch a break. First, he breaks up with Carlos, now he has a crazy stalker. If anyone really could use a big hunky man like Carlos in his life right now, it's my buddy Chris.*

Chapter Fourteen

Loath though he was to admit it, Martin was beginning to realise he needed help to track the vampire. The kid, Chris, had managed to escape from him again. He would have gotten him if the cop hadn't been so damned handy, but he'd sensed something different about Chris this time around. Martin had inherited a gift from his grandmother. An instinctual perception which, although he had never tried to understand it or improve on it, had been invaluable to him on occasion when dealing with paranormal situations. In his confrontation with Chris earlier in the day, he'd realised that not only did the kid not know his friend was a vampire, he was now no longer aware of their friendship.

Their friendship had been erased from his mind.

Which could only mean one thing. The vampire had revealed himself, and the kid had freaked. He could thank his lucky stars his memory was the only thing the vampire had taken. Sometimes, they ended up a blood sandwich. The vampire must have really liked the kid, and that was a good thing, because it meant Martin could still use Chris to get to him.

And something else he'd been aware of — all too aware of — that knee to the groin had really hurt. The kid was stronger and faster than he should be for his height and weight. Not nearly as strong as a full-fledged vampire, but he'd bet there had been blood involved, whether Chris knew it or not. That meant the vampire was closely attuned to the kid, and again, that would work in Martin's favour. Martin was pretty sure that if Chris was in any real danger, El Nosferatu would come flying to the rescue — and this time, he, Martin, wouldn't make any mistakes.

Pulling out his cell phone, he punched in a number he knew by heart.

"Vince? Martin here, how are you?"

"Good. Whatcha got?"

"I'm in LA tracking a bloodsucker. I got close once, but he's strong, plus some fool got in the way."

"That was careless, Martin."

"I know that," Martin snapped.

"What happened to the so-called ESP you're so damned proud of — or is that so much bullshit, like the rest of your stories?"

"It won't happen again," Martin snapped, ignoring Vince's insult. "I need help on this one, so are you available?"

"Okay, but to remedy an aborted attempt, I charge more."

"What do you mean 'charge'? You're supposed to be my partner. How much more?"

"Seventy-five percent of the bounty."

"That's outrageous."

"Take it or leave it."

Martin ground his teeth as he listened to Vince's loud yawn of feigned disinterest. "All right, it's a deal."

"Too easy, Martin," Vince snickered. "Too quick to accept. You'll try and cut me out once the job is done. Whatcha got in the bank?"

"You want payment upfront? That's unheard of."

"Until now. I know you, Martin—ergo, I don't trust you. After all, you didn't tell me you were on the hunt until you blew it and needed my help. Am I right?"

"Forget it," Martin snarled.

"Suit yourself." The line went dead.

"Son-of-a-bitch!" Martin snapped closed his cell phone. Instinctively, he knew Vince wouldn't leave it there. Now he was aware there was a vampire to be caught, he'd be in LA within a few hours—and Vince was good. Martin cursed under his breath. On top of the kid being as slippery as an eel, now he'd have to contend with Vince trying to get to the vampire first. Damn it all to hell!

* * * *

Billy woke, feeling like he'd been run over by a fire engine. Every bone in his body ached like they were being squeezed in a metal vice, and his head hurt so bad it was painful just to open his eyes. When he did force them open, the first thing he saw was Frank's sourpuss, and he quickly shut them again.

"Wake up, Billy." Frank's nasal whine grated on Billy's overly sensitive hearing.

"Oh, man, I feel like shit," Billy moaned.

"I got some coffee goin', but I ain't no butler, so get up and help yourself. Then we need to talk."

Fuck. Billy knew he shouldn't have asked Frank if he could stay just one more night, but he'd hurt all over—still did. But now, Frank wanted something for letting him stay the extra night. "What about?" he asked, struggling off the couch.

"The kid from the Xtasy Club. You know where he lives, right?"

"What about it?"

"I want you to show me where the little prick hangs out, so you and me can go over there and get him while his big friend is nowhere around."

Billy poured himself a mug of coffee. "His big friend is a vampire, Frank, and I ain't goin' anywheres near him again."

"Vampire, shmampire, Billy. I told you, there's no such thing." Frank waved a hand dismissively. "And besides, I just said we'd get the kid when the big guy isn't around."

"That would have to be in the daytime then."

Frank sighed with exasperation. "The *daytime*? We're just gonna walk up there in broad daylight, let him see us comin' so he can call the cops? What are you, nuts?"

"But, Frank," Billy quavered. "Vampires can't come out in the daytime."

"Shut the fuck up about vampires!" Frank's face grew purple with frustrated rage. "Once and for all, there is no such thing!"

"You're wrong, Frank." Billy sat on the couch and started to pull on his shoes. "I know what I saw with my own eyes, and that was no human being who got stabbed in the back and still had the strength to pick me up and throw me off the balcony. And that asshole vampire hunter wouldn't be no use either. If you don't believe me, and you want the kid so bad, *you* go get him by yourself."

"So give me the address, Billy," Frank snarled. "I can handle that punk kid all by myself."

"Good luck with that. He lives in Weho, corner of Sequoia and Spruce, second floor." Billy glared at his soon to be ex-buddy through jaundice-yellow eyes. "One day, Frank, you'll wish you'd listened to me about all this. Go near that kid, and you'll be sorry."

"Fuck off!"

"I intend doing just that," Billy muttered, pushing himself off the couch. "I'm outta here!"

Frank slumped back in his chair as Billy marched out through the door, slamming it behind him. "What a dumb schmuck," he muttered. "What a loser."

* * * *

Nightfall, and Carlos was anxious to make certain Chris was not being stalked by the vampire hunter or perhaps by the men in the alley out seeking revenge for the beating he had inflicted on them. Blending in with the shadows cast by the tall trees that lined the street, he stared across at the apartment building and felt better on realising Chris was not at home. His mind reached out to touch Chris' thoughts, and he smiled sadly as his consciousness picked up Chris' laughter and animated conversation.

"He's with a friend," he murmured and tried to feel good about that. They had been apart only one day, but it was the thought of the endless days to come when they would still be apart that filled his heart with grief. He stiffened as he saw some movement near Chris' door.

Not the hunter, he instinctively knew. Someone clumsy, malicious, intent on doing damage. Soundlessly, he glided across the street and up the steps that led to Chris' front door. A man, crouched over and completely oblivious to Carlos' presence, tried to jimmy the door open.

"Can I help you?"

Frank gave out a startled yelp of fear and jumped a good foot off the ground. He fell over onto his hands and knees, the metal jimmy skittering towards Carlos, who picked it up, and tossed it over the side of the steps.

"I don't think you will need that anymore, do you?"

Frank got slowly to his feet, his eyes casting about for the best direction in which to run. He looked up at Carlos. Shit. It was the guy from the alley. He'd never be able to put this one down, even if he still had the jimmy in his hand—which he didn't.

"I, uh, locked myself out," he croaked.

"You are a liar. I know who lives here, and I know you were planning some mischief."

Frank quaked visibly. This guy was totally scary. In the alley, he'd looked tall, but Frank didn't remember him being *this* tall or so *fierce* looking.

"Me? No, no...I must have been trying the wrong door." Frank attempted to laugh, but it came out more like a choked sob. "Okay, just let me go. I won't come back, I swear."

"I know you won't come back." Carlos reached for Frank, grabbed him by his coat collar and lifted him off the ground. Frank squealed with fear. Carlos walked to the edge of the steps then raised himself into the air.

"*No*," Frank screamed. "This can't be happening!"

"But it is happening," Carlos murmured, picking up some speed.

Frank writhed and struggled in Carlos' grasp, until he heard his coat rip. "*No*! Don't let me fall. Please don't let me fall!"

And Carlos did let him fall then caught up with the screaming man as he plummeted towards the hard, unyielding ground below, grabbing him again by the scruff of his neck. Frank finally stopped screaming. He had passed out. Carlos set him down on a stretch of desert several hundred miles from Los Angeles then settled down on his haunches and waited for him to regain consciousness. Whimpering as he came round, Frank stared at him, eyes stark with fear when they focused on Carlos.

"Billy was right," he croaked. "You're a...you're a—"

"Vampire," Carlos finished for him. "Yes, Billy was right and was afraid, just as you should now be." He grabbed the lapels of Frank's coat and drew him near. His nostrils flared with disgust at the smell of Frank's urine. The man had peed his pants. Over Frank's almost incoherent pleas for mercy, he said, "Perhaps now you will leave Christopher alone. For if you do not, next time, I promise you I will not be so kind." He let Frank fall back from his grip and stood, towering over the quivering man. "Do you understand?"

"Yes, yes." Frank grovelled at Carlos' feet. His jaw went slack as Carlos lifted himself into the air and flew away, leaving Frank alone in the dark and very far from home.

* * * *

"So, what are we going to do about this situation?" Roger asked Micah. The two of them were leaving a Beverly Centre multiplex where they had just seen a rerun of *Shadow of the Vampire*.

"You mean the vampire hunter?" Micah asked. "I thought Marcus, Joseph and Carlos were dealing with that."

Roger frowned. "I guess we should all be dealing with it, but I meant the situation with Carlos and Chris."

"What can we do about that? Carlos has erased himself from Chris' memory. We can't change that."

"Who says?"

"Joseph says," Micah said, chuckling. "We were talking about this last night. Carlos gave Chris his blood. They were bonded because of that, but Carlos severed the bond, and only he can fix it."

"Damn," Roger muttered. "I was hoping you and I could maybe go see Chris and —"

"Are you nuts?" Micah stared at him in disbelief. "Do you know what trouble we'd be in if we interfered in this? Sometimes Roger, you are just too much."

"Well, I've tried talking to Carlos, and he won't do anything 'cept roam about, making sure Chris is okay. The guy's hurting. He's in love, Micah."

"I know he is, and the situation stinks, Roger, but we can't go trying to change things. We might make it a lot worse. By the way, Joseph told me the Vampire Council informed him that the vampire hunter, Martin Kellogg, is one of only four actively hunting vampires in the States. He and some other guy, Vince LaGuardia, usually work together, but Kellogg is loning it this time."

"So he hasn't any backup?"

"No. And from what Carlos told us about Chris getting the better of him a couple of times, he's not very smart."

"Hmm, that's encouraging," Roger muttered. He grabbed Micah's arm. "Hey look, isn't that Chris with some dude up ahead?"

"Yes, it is. They must have been at the flicks, too."

Roger frowned. "Could he have hooked up with someone else already?"

"It could be just a friend, Roger. And remember, he has no memory of Carlos." They watched as Joey and Chris, deep in conversation, sauntered towards the movie house parking lot then Micah gave Roger a wary look. "You've gone quiet. What are you planning?"

"Something devious," Roger replied. "Something that will get us into a lot of trouble if we're found out."

"Oh no," Micah muttered. "I just got a flash—"

"Well, we have to feed. If we do this right then we'll be connected to Chris."

"No, Roger."

"Okay, you do the other guy. I'll take Chris."

"*Roger.*"

But Roger had gone, disappearing in a preternatural blur of movement no human eye could see. Despite his better judgement, and because in about one second flat Chris' buddy would start screaming blue-bloody murder, he dove after Roger faster than a speeding bullet.

* * * *

Chris was just about to open his car door when strong arms wrapped around him and he was lifted off his feet at an alarming speed. Before he could even yell, he saw Joey disappear then Chris was literally flying through the air, supported by a young man who looked vaguely familiar. They landed somewhere—Chris had no idea where, nor did he have time to wonder. He couldn't tear his eyes from the young man's powerful gaze. He felt drawn to him in a way he couldn't quite understand and didn't mind at all when the stranger laid a trail of kisses up the curve of his jaw before his lips nuzzled at Chris' throat.

Chris arched his neck, enjoying the feel of lips and teeth working at his skin. *I'm going to have a big old hickey in the morning, but who cares? This feels so good...* He cupped the back of the man's head and wound his fingers into the thick blond curls.

The sting of a bite made him wince, but his moan of pain was quickly transformed into one of ecstasy as his body was suffused in a white-hot heat of desire. His erection pressed against the man's thigh.

Chris felt a tug of disappointment when the man pulled back then again was mesmerised by the sparkling, dark-blue gaze that met his own wide-eyed stare.

"Christopher…"

"Do I know you?" Chris asked shakily.

The young man lowered his head over his wrist and when he brought it to Chris' lips it oozed dark-red blood. Without hesitation, as if were the most natural thing in the world for him to do, Chris lapped at the blood, relishing every drop of the rich, dark, spicy flavour.

"Look at me," the blond man said, removing his wrist from Chris' lips. Obediently, Chris looked into the young man's eyes and saw not the fresh-faced California blond but a vision of a tall, darkly handsome man. Memories stirred in Chris' mind. Wonderful memories of times spent with this man, times of rapture, of yearning and complete fulfilment.

"Remember him," the young man whispered. "His name is Carlos Galeano."

* * * *

Chris opened his car door and sank into the seat next to Joey. His friend turned to him and gave him a drowsy smile.

"Did we just have sex?" he asked, his eyes slightly unfocused.

"I...I don't think so," Chris stammered. "At...at least not with each other. I think his name was Carlos."

Joey sat bolt upright in his seat, the smile wiped from his face. "Carlos? *Your* Carlos?"

Chris stared at Joey with complete bafflement. "*My* Carlos?"

"The guy you were dating. The one you just broke up with. The Spanish guy who offered you a job. The guy you were nuts about for Chrissakes."

"Joey! I don't know what the hell you're talking about."

Joey groaned and sank back into his seat. "What are you, suddenly? The Queen of denial? For Pete's sake Chris, you were ranting and raving about Carlos practically all the way up to Santa Barbara. You told your folks you were going to be working for him—antiques or somethin'. Then a couple of days ago you told me you'd split up—or no, wait a minute, you didn't actually say that. You said there was no Carlos in your life. I just assumed you'd split up. And now here you go again with the 'Carlos who?' routine."

Chris shook his head slowly. "Honestly Joey, I don't know what you're talking about." He turned the key in the ignition and put the car in gear. "All I know is," he said, reversing out of the parking bay, "I just had a vision of this really hot guy whose name is Carlos. It was like I did know him. But date him? Work for him? I don't think so."

"That's it," Joey grunted. "I am officially dubbing you the airhead of all time. You wanna play these silly games, go ahead. Just don't include me in them."

"Joey, honestly..."

"Don't start that again," Joey snapped. He let his head fall back onto the headrest and closed his eyes. "I just want to try and remember what happened earlier. Some guy with the sweetest mouth…" He put his hand to his neck in a reflex movement. "If I don't have a hickey in the morning, I'll be surprised."

Instinctively, Chris put a hand to his neck. Yeah, that's what he'd thought, too. What the hell had happened earlier? The vision of a tall man with dark, golden-brown, brooding eyes swam before him, momentarily blocking out the glare of the oncoming traffic's headlights.

Remember him, a voice echoed in his mind. *His name is Carlos Galeano.*

Chapter Fifteen

After Chris dropped a still slightly miffed Joey at his apartment, he headed home, feeling an almost overpowering need to be alone. Joey hadn't put up too much of an argument when Chris said he wouldn't stay over with him after all. They had both felt a bit dazed and confused about what had happened after they left the movie house. Something wonderful—but what the hell had it been? He pulled into his parking spot and looked around warily for any sign of the nutcase who had accosted him in the morning, but it all looked clear and quiet outside the apartment.

Besides, he thought, walking up the steps to his front door, *that guy shows up again, I may just knock his lights out.* In contrast to how he'd felt earlier, he was now experiencing a sense of vigour and well being—strong. He chuckled, half hoping the guy would actually jump out of the shadows, and he could put him away but good. Poised on the top step and pulling his key out of his pocket, he looked around, staring into the dimly lit grounds that surrounded the apartment building.

Was someone watching him? His skin prickled as he scanned the darkly shadowed trees on the other side of the street. Was that a shadow or the figure of a tall man standing there? It couldn't be the crazy man — too tall for him. Chris narrowed his eyes, focusing in on the figure. It was definitely a man, he decided, slightly startled that he could see so clearly in the dark and at such a distance. What was going on with him? He felt different somehow — more alert, more aware of the sights and sounds of the night.

The man started to move away.

No, don't go. I want to know who you are.

Chris ran down the steps and across the street at a speed he hadn't known he was capable of, but even so he was too late. The man was gone. A feeling of desolation swept over Chris, a feeling he couldn't for the life of him understand. Why would he be saddened by a stranger's disappearance? It made no sense. He didn't know the man, yet he'd had an overwhelming desire to be close to him, to speak to him, to put his arms around him and press his face to the man's chest —

Whoa. Where the hell were these crazy thoughts coming from?

"Go home, Chris," he muttered to himself. *Yeah, go home and go to bed, and tomorrow call your folks and tell them you're really coming home — for good.*

Carlos watched as Chris walked back across the street, through the parking lot then up the steps to his apartment. He'd read Chris' thoughts and was saddened by his decision to go back to Santa Barbara. But there was something else there in Chris' mind. A confusion but, fortunately, no fear. He'd had an experience that had not been at all unpleasant, but the memory of just what that experience had been still eluded him. Carlos already knew what had occurred, but who among the vampires in LA could it have been?

He probed Chris' mind for a name, a face, though it was unlikely he would remember either one. Chris disappeared inside his apartment, and Carlos raised himself into the air, gliding across to the building, landing lightly on the balcony. He saw Chris move about the living room, pour himself a glass of wine, take a sip then walk into the bedroom. Carlos watched with longing as Chris pulled off his shirt and jeans, revealing his slender, toned body—the body Carlos could no longer hold and caress.

Wearing only his briefs, Chris walked back into the living room, picked up his glass of wine from the kitchen counter then flopped down on the couch where he sat staring up at the ceiling. Carlos felt his frustration as he tried to remember the elusive events of the evening. He stiffened with surprise as Chris closed his eyes and brought a vision of a man's face to the forefront of his mind.

"*Dios,*" he murmured. "*Esta mio.* It's *me* he's remembering." For the words he heard so clearly in Chris' mind were, *Remember him. His name is Carlos Galeano.*

Who had done this? Who of all the vampires in LA he knew personally would have done this? Not with malice. He sensed that. Chris' mind was calm, questioning, trying so hard to remember — *longing* to remember. Someone had interfered, hoping perhaps to bring a reconciliation between Chris and himself. He smiled ruefully. Only one he knew would be this headstrong and foolish — well intentioned, perhaps, but foolish.

Roger.

Carlos sighed. He would appear ungrateful if he berated Roger for this, and Marcus would no doubt be furious with his young lover. He did not want to cause a rift between them, but he could not allow Roger to think he was being helpful in this matter. Chris' memories should not be tampered with in this way.

It was bad enough that I made him forget what had really happened in the alleyway then let him remember when he would not believe I was a vampire, only to erase all memories of our time together, Carlos thought with sadness. *And now Roger, thinking that he was doing the right thing, has brought me to Christopher's awareness again.*

Carlos passed his hand over the sliding glass door lock, sealing it from outside entry then, knowing that Chris would be safe here for yet another night, he rose into the air, heading back to his friends' house in Hollywood Hills.

Chris drank the last of his wine then pulled a pillow behind his head and stretched out on the couch. What a weird night this has been, he reflected, and doubly weird that Joey seemed to have had much the same experience. *And why the hell does he keep insisting I know a guy named Carlos?*

Carlos. Carlos Galeano. Why did that name sound so familiar? When he closed his eyes, he saw a vision of the man who had appeared in his mind during that earlier, almost out-of-the-body experience.

"Carlos," he whispered, seeing again the dark, beguiling eyes, the mane of black hair, the sensuous smile. *Who are you, Carlos? I wish I could remember more about you, how we met, what we meant to one another... Why can't I remember?*

He was just beginning to doze off when he heard a loud knocking at his door.

"Who the—? Oh, bet that's Joey."

* * * *

"Roger." Micah's voice was tense with worry. "Carlos isn't going to appreciate you messing with Chris like this."

Roger smiled as he sank back into the cushioned patio chair. "Oh, yeah. He'll appreciate it when Chris remembers the great times he had with Carlos and doesn't mind at all that he was doing it with a vampire."

"Roger, how on earth are you going to do that? I know you've connected with him, but you're a novice at this kind of thing. It takes someone like Marcus or Joseph—or Carlos himself—to do what you're attempting, and you know Carlos would never go for it."

"Listen, you and I have the most powerful vampire strain around," Roger reminded him. "It comes directly from Marcus, and his powers are awesome, as you know."

"Right, but he's had years to perfect them. *Hundreds of years* as you like to point out on occasion. He *knows* what he's doing."

"I know what I'm doing," Roger said, pouting. "I'm taking it nice and slow, just a hint at a time. Just a flash of Carlos now and then—and let me tell you, Chris is very receptive."

"You think he's beginning to remember?"

"He remembers something. He's just not quite sure of the how and the why."

"Supposing it all comes back too quickly, and he freaks when he remembers Carlos is a vampire? It might tip him over the edge."

Micah jumped slightly when Marcus and Joseph suddenly appeared on the veranda.

"Why have you closed your minds to Joseph and I?" Marcus demanded, his eyes riveted on Roger. "What are you up to now?"

Roger looked beyond them warily. "Is Carlos with you?"

"No, he hasn't yet returned, and..." Marcus paused, his eyes narrowing. "Oh, Roger, Micah, you didn't—"

"It wasn't my idea," Micah yelped. "Roger said it would help Carlos."

"Traitor," Roger muttered. He pushed himself to his feet, trying to look more nonchalant than he felt. "Look, guys, Carlos is all lost and lonely. He's trying to act the macho man, like it doesn't matter, but you can see it in his eyes, sense it in his demeanour. He's hurting, and Micah and I just wanted to help."

Joseph put his arm around Micah's shoulders and hugged him to his side. "That is a very nice thought," he said in his husky tones. "But you really should not be interfering in matters like these. Carlos made the decision to have Christopher forget him. To try to change that without Carlos' consent is invading his privacy."

"You think he'll be mad at us?" Micah asked.

"Undoubtedly," Marcus said, his gaze still fixed on Roger. "Have you thought of the consequences of your actions?"

Roger shrugged. "Well, what I'm hoping for is that Chris and Carlos will be reunited. Isn't that what we all want? The guy's thinking of leaving for Santa Barbara tomorrow — probably for good."

"Then that is how it must end," Marcus said. "You will not meddle in this again."

Roger pushed out his lower lip defiantly. "But this is crazy," he blurted. "Marcus, you of all the vampires in the world, could make this right. You did it for Micah and Joseph — why not for Carlos?"

Marcus sighed. "That was different. Joseph was in danger at the time. I merely sowed the seed in Micah's mind that when they next met, he would know what Joseph was. I didn't have time to ask Joseph's permission."

"And it worked out great," Roger interrupted. "So why not for Carlos and Chris?"

"Because, as I have already stated, Carlos has made his own decision. If he had wanted our help, he would have asked for it, and of course, I would have given it gladly."

"What if you offered?"

"I have offered, but he wanted Christopher to come to him of his own free will, not coerced by vampire magic."

"Well, damn," Roger muttered, looking decidedly mutinous.

"Enough now." Marcus looked back inside the house. "Carlos is here." He turned to look again at Roger. "Promise me you will not attempt to interfere again. As well intentioned as your actions are, Carlos will not welcome them."

"But—"

"Roger." Marcus put his hands on Roger's shoulders and locked eyes with him. "Promise me."

Roger sighed and put his head on Marcus' chest. "I promise," he mumbled.

Micah couldn't resist checking to make sure Roger's fingers weren't crossed behind Marcus' back. His attention was drawn to Carlos' handsome figure as he stepped onto the veranda.

"Hi, Carlos."

Carlos inclined his head, smiling at Micah and Joseph before his gaze swept over Marcus and Roger still in each other's arms. "Am I interrupting?" he asked.

"Not at all," Marcus replied, disengaging himself from Roger's embrace. He took in his friend's sombre expression. "Are you all right?"

"*Si, gracias.* I have just come from Christopher's apartment, making sure he was safe for the night. He plans on leaving soon for his home in Santa Barbara."

"I am sorry, my friend," Marcus murmured.

"It is perhaps for the best."

"But—" Roger started to object. Marcus gripped his arm warning him not to say what was on his mind, and for a moment or two, there was a slightly uncomfortable silence amongst the friends. Carlos regarded Roger for a beat longer, and when he smiled, it did not quite reach his eyes.

"I know that what you did, Roger," he said quietly, "was done with the best of intentions and, I am sure, with my happiness in mind. But I must ask you to please sever the blood bond you've formed with Christopher and let our destinies be as they were intended." His gaze flicked to Marcus as he continued, "I shall return to Madrid as soon as I have dealt with the hunter, Martin Kellogg."

"But Carlos," Roger blurted. "Why give up so easily? Look, I know what I did was out of line, and I apologise for that, but I'm telling you Chris is the guy for you. I saw how he reacted to the memory of you."

"*Roger.*" Marcus squeezed Roger's biceps tightly until the younger vampire winced. "You promised me you would no longer interfere in this matter—now let it go. Carlos must decide what it best for him and Christopher, not you."

Roger slumped against Marcus' powerful body. "All right, all right. But it just pisses me off that Carlos is being such a wuss about this."

"*Roger.*" Marcus stared at him in shock.

"Excuse me?" Carlos, who was not short in stature to begin with, seemed to grow taller as he bridled at Roger's insult.

"Oh boy," Micah muttered.

"Well, I'm sorry." Roger's tone was defiant and not at all sorry. "You're just so ready to walk away from him because you can't stand the thought of having to deal with his terror of what you are, of what we *all* are. But I'm telling you this, Chris was in love with you and could be again, if you handle it right."

"That's enough, Roger," Marcus snapped.

Anything further that Roger or Carlos might have said was stayed as a muffled cry for help reached both their minds.

"Chris — topher," they said simultaneously.

Micah looked at them with alarm. "What is it?"

"Someone's got him," Roger said.

"But I sealed his apartment from the outside."

"He might have opened the door —"

Marcus raised himself into the air. "Let's not waste time. Carlos, lead the way. We will follow!"

Chapter Sixteen

Vince LaGuardia pushed Martin aside with an angry grunt of impatience. "You're telling me you couldn't take this kid on your own? Call yourself a hunter, Martin? You're less than worthless."

Martin seethed with rage beside him. "You just got lucky, that's all. You were fortunate he was half asleep when he answered the door." He looked down at Chris' unconscious, bound and gagged body. "Let's get the hell out of here before his vampire friend figures out we've got him. We have to be the ones with the advantage."

Vince glanced at Martin's sweating face and sneered. "Scared, Martin?"

"No, just careful. The vampire's strong, stronger than any you or I have dealt with in the past. We shouldn't hang around here. Let's get the kid over to the base. There, we have the advantage."

His one time partner snickered as he hoisted Chris off the couch and over his shoulder. "You're scared," he rasped, his eyes showing contempt. "Okay, let's go." He headed for the door, Martin following close behind. Once outside, they made for Vince's vehicle, a black Oldsmobile SUV. Throwing Chris in the back, the men wasted no time, gunning the Olds, lights out, down the street. Martin twisted round to peer out the rear window, and his jaw dropped open as he saw five dark shapes descending from the night sky outside Chris' apartment building.

"Holy Christ, Vince. He's brought reinforcements."

"What are you talking about?"

"There's at least five of the bastards back there."

Vince swore under his breath. "You didn't know he had friends? What kind of research did you do? You and your *instinctual perception*. What did you do? Switch off your fucking brain?" He swore again as Martin remained silent. "You're not going to be hunting much longer at this rate, Martin. You're going to get yourself killed, and me along with you if they get to us first. Shit! I never should've listened to you." He punched the accelerator hard, entering the freeway that led to downtown at breakneck speed. "Let's just hope we make it to base before they pick up his scent."

"Maybe we should just ditch him," Martin muttered.

Vince shook his head vigorously. "Uh-uh. Even if we let him go, they won't let up 'til they find us. The kid's our leverage. We've come this far, we'll see it through. Keep your eyes peeled for any sign of them."

Nervously, Martin dropped his window and peered out again, his eyes scanning the cloud-covered sky above them. "Nothing," he mumbled, turning to look at Chris who glared at him from the backseat. "Kid's conscious," he told Vince.

"Good. Means I don't have to carry him again," Vince said, chuckling.

Martin glanced at him, shivering at the intensity that gripped the other hunter. He knew Vince was just crazy enough to try to take on all five vampires. He was arrogant, considering himself invincible and a match for anything the undead threw against him. It was true he'd had considerable success hunting vampires in the past. He'd collected several bounties over the years, but they'd been mostly for young vampires, newly changed and unaware of the full potential of their powers. The vampire Martin had gone against the other night was different—strong enough to survive even with a silver blade buried in his back. Martin shuddered again at the memory of how close he'd come to being killed. Now, the possibility was even greater, especially if Vince was nuts enough to try taking out all five at the same time.

No way could it happen, and yet...

His greedy mind couldn't resist the thought of what it would mean if they managed to pull it off. *Man, five bounties.* Even if he had to share with Vince, he'd be set for life. He licked his lips at the thought of the money. His eyes darted to the sign that told him they had reached the downtown exit. He stuck his head out the window for a last look around. Still nothing. They might just do this.

Vince pulled the SUV into a dark side street and brought it to a screeching halt outside an unlit doorway.

"Out, quick," he yelled at Martin, flinging himself out of the car. He yanked open the passenger door and hauled Chris out, pushing him towards the doorway. "Hurry it up," he rasped. Martin unlocked the door and three of them stumbled inside. Vince slammed the door behind them, quickly saying the words that sealed it against uninvited entry. The building they used as a 'hunter base' was not anyone's home, never had been, therefore they could not bar entry to a vampire or other supernatural force without the hunter incantation.

"That should hold them 'til we're ready," Vince muttered.

* * * *

Chris looked around the dingy room, a feeling of despair clutching at his stomach. He shivered from the cold air, realising he wore only his briefs. *What the hell did these madmen think they were doing?* He felt bewildered by all that had happened in the past few hours. What possible reason could they have for taking him to this godforsaken place?

The one named Martin looked nervous, but his partner Vince was another kind of man altogether. Tall and well built, handsome in a rough sort of way, he looked determined — and dangerous. Chris glared as Vince pushed him down onto a chair and lifted the gag from his mouth.

"Your buddies will be here soon," he said, his ice-cold eyes locked on Chris'. "They'll follow your blood scent and come straight here."

"Blood scent?" Chris stared at him. "What the hell are you talking about?"

"He doesn't know what's been done to him," Martin said, snickering. "Doesn't know he's slept with a vampire and drunk vampire blood."

"You're both nuts," Chris gasped.

"No." Vince grabbed Chris' hair and tilted his head back, staring even harder into his eyes. "We're not nuts. We're vampire hunters, and we have you here as bait. Pretty soon your vampire lover and his cronies will try to get in here to rescue you, but we have a couple of surprises for them." His eyes widened, and he jumped back, releasing his grip on Chris' hair as a tremendous crash shook the building.

"Christ," Martin yelped, then yelped again as another crash seemed to shake the building to its foundations.

"They can't get in," Vince snarled at him.

"They won't have to, if they knock down the fucking building," Martin rasped back.

Chris gaped up at the two men. What was happening? Whatever it was, these two were going to be no use to him if whatever or whoever actually managed to destroy the building. He struggled with the ropes that tied his hands behind his back. He stiffened as he heard a deep and melodious voice inside his mind telling him to be calm and not be afraid.

Who…?

Christopher, I must reveal myself to you again. My name is Carlos, and you are going to remember me now, and all that we've meant to one another. Don't be afraid, querido.

Chris' mind was flooded with images of himself and a beautiful, dark-haired man locked in an embrace, their lips joined in an all-consuming kiss. Chris felt his body suffused by a sensual heat that brought back myriad memories of nights spent in the man's arms, of whispered conversations, of sweet longing, of total fulfilment—and a revelation that had torn them apart. Only now, he understood, and he was not afraid.

"Carlos," he murmured. Closing his eyes he gave himself up to the rapture that coursed through his body setting his blood on fire with desire—and strength. With a final wrench, he broke free of the ropes that bound him.

Martin's eyes fairly bugged out of his head when Chris jumped to his feet. "Vince!" he yelled. "The kid's snapped the ropes—the vampire blood's made him even stronger. Shit!" His words were lost in a violent rending sound as the ceiling above them began to peel back. "Jesus, Vince, do *something*!"

"You know the words as well as I do," Vince yelled at him. "Start saying them now while I take care of the kid." He darted across the room to where Chris stood staring about him, looking for a way out. Chris picked up the chair he been tied to and swung it at Vince's head as the man tried to grab him. The chair hit Vince's shoulder, slowing him down, and he cursed out loud reaching for Chris as he ran for the door, pulling so hard on the knob it came free in his hand. He turned and threw it at Vince, the metal glancing off the hunter's skull, bringing a screech of pain and rage from his throat.

Martin's nervous, quavering voice stuttered out a chant of what sounded like Latin phrases to Chris.

"Louder, you idiot," Vince screamed, holding his forehead and joining in.

"*Mucronia, bisulcumis, forare, morderemus...*" There was a slight pause then their words were cut off as another ear-splitting crash reverberated overhead, and a deluge of wood and plaster rained down on top of them, causing the hunters to run for cover.

"It's not working," Martin whimpered. "They're going to get in."

Outside, the vampires surrounded them, their collective powers slowly destroying the building, brick by brick and overcoming the hunter's attempt to use ancient magic against them. Carlos sensed exactly where Chris was and was careful to deflect any falling debris from him.

"Carlos," Marcus called out. "The seal has been broken. You can get Christopher out now."

Carlos nodded and, in one blurred movement, was at the door, flinging it open with a wave of his hand. His smile was one of cold satisfaction at the sight of the two hunters huddled together in a corner, arms raised to protect themselves from the timber and tile that still fell all around them. His gaze moved to Chris who stood unharmed by the door, his expression one of recognition and love.

Soundlessly, he moved into Carlos' arms, burying his head against the hard, welcoming chest. Carlos held him, fusing their bodies together in an embrace that at any other time neither man would have wanted to end. They were almost unaware of the four figures entering what remained of the room to confront the hunters, their vampire faces pale and hard in the moonlight that slanted through the ruined roof.

Slowly the hunters got to their feet, Martin visibly quaking, Vince affecting a defiant stance. "Safety in numbers, eh, vampires?" he sneered. "What? It takes all of you to have the courage to face us?"

Marcus exchanged an amused look with Joseph then, without a word, they stretched out their right hands and levitated both Martin and Vince until their heads disappeared through the gap in the ceiling. The hunters' bodies twisted and writhed in futile attempts to stop themselves from rising further into the air until finally Martin shrieked out a plea for mercy. Abruptly, Marcus dropped his arm and Martin plummeted to the ground where he lay dazed and groaning.

"What do you say, hunter?" Joseph taunted Vince who still struggled in midair. "Will you meet me in combat?"

"Let me down, and you'll find out."

Joseph lowered his arm slowly, allowing Vince to land on his feet then he strode forward and gripped Vince by the throat, bringing the hunter's face to within an inch of his own.

"Your kind have murdered friends of mine throughout the ages," he hissed, his fangs extended. "But never in combat, only in cowardly attacks during the daylight hours. Now here's your chance to show your courage, hunter. Draw your weapon and face me." He flung Vince away from him, allowing the man to draw his silver-bladed knife from inside his coat.

"And if I kill you, will the others let me live?" Vince asked, his tongue flicking nervously over his lower lip.

Joseph's smile was wicked. "They might. But first you will have to kill me, then negotiate."

Chris, who had been watching this scene unfold before his astounded eyes, looked up at Carlos' grim expression. So it was true. This beautiful man holding him in his arms, along with the four men he now recognised and whose names he remembered, were vampires. What Carlos had revealed to him on that fateful night, the last time they had been together, what he had forgotten until now, was all true. It was incredible, but what was even more incredible was that he was unafraid. Instinctively, he knew that he had much more to fear from the two vampire hunters than from Carlos and his friends. They had come to save him, and now, Joseph might be killed.

Carlos' arm tightened around him. "Joseph is in no danger," he murmured. "The hunter is cunning, but he is no match for any of us — when we are awake."

Vince lunged forward, his knife raking the air in front of Joseph, missing his throat by a mere inch. Joseph feinted then stepped back, grabbing Vince's wrist, twisting it slowly until with a moan of pain, Vince let the knife fall from his hand. He stood facing Joseph, a visible shudder of fear rippling through his body. Joseph released the hunter's wrist then placed a hand on either side of Vince's face, drawing him close into what was almost a lover's embrace, staring intently into his eyes.

"What's he doing?" Chris asked in a whisper.

"He is finding another path for the hunter's journey through life."

"What does that mean?"

"Watch."

Vince stumbled backwards as Joseph released him. He looked around the ruined room, an expression of complete bewilderment on his face.

"What's going on?" he asked.

"You seem to have strayed in here by mistake," Joseph told him.

"No, no!" Martin leapt to his feet, grabbing at Vince's arm. "They're tricking you, Vince. They're vampires. Don't you remember? We came here to kill them."

Vince stared at Martin then slowly shook his head. "You're insane, man. I don't even know who you are." He pulled himself free of Martin's grip. "Guess I'll be on my way then. Sorry if I interrupted something."

"Don't leave me here with them," Martin wailed. "They're vampires!"

Vince gave Joseph a sad smile, shrugged then walked from the room onto the dark street outside. Moments later, the sound of his SUV's engine starting had Martin trying to run from the room in pursuit of his ex-partner. Carlos reached out and grabbed him, practically lifting the panicked man off his feet.

The others gathered around Martin, and Chris began to feel real pity for the man who had been stalking him. Then he remembered the savage attack on Carlos, the knife buried deep in his back, the blood, all of that horror flooding his mind as the events of the past several days became clear and stark in his memory. His pity turned to anger.

Martin fell on his knees in front of Carlos. The vampire hunter's worst nightmare was unfolding around him. Alone, with five vampires and a mortal who now stared down at him with cold and unforgiving eyes.

"Please," he whimpered. "I'm alone and unarmed. This was all Vincent LaGuardia's idea. You let *him* go..." He cringed as the vampires chuckled, sinister sounds that echoed in the barren room, completely without mirth. "Please," he cried again. "I'll just go away, disappear. You'll never see or hear from me again."

"It would be better," Marcus rasped, "if all of humanity never saw or heard of you again."

"Right," Roger added. "You really are a worthless piece o' shit, you know."

"Totally worthless," Micah muttered.

"So, what shall we do with him?" Joseph asked.

Marcus smiled. "Carlos?"

Carlos pulled Martin to his feet then pushed him into Joseph's arms. "Kill him," he said.

"No, no, no!" Martin whirled away out of Joseph's waiting embrace and ran smack into Marcus who snapped at him, fangs flashing. Hysterical now, Martin tried again to run for the door, but this time Roger and Micah grabbed him and led him back in front of Carlos. "Please, no..."

Chris tugged on Carlos' arm. "Carlos, he's scared enough."

Carlos grinned at him, showing just the tips of his fangs. "You think? Then I'll let you decide his fate."

"Just do what Joseph did to the other one," Chris said. "That seemed to work okay."

"Boring," Roger protested. "I say we carve him up!"

"Ugh, no." Micah grimaced. "You want *that* blood in you? Yuck."

"Please," Martin whimpered again.

"Oh, for the love of the gods," Joseph muttered. "Do *something*, Carlos. His constant pleading is bad for my nerves."

"If you insist." Carlos reached for Martin and lifted him up with one hand on the hunter's collar until their eyes were level with each other. "You have no idea how I have longed for this moment," Carlos said, his voice low and venomous. "There was a time when I dreamed of all the many ways I could make one of your kind suffer. To make you pay, as it were, for the death of a loved one, and now that I have you here in my grasp..." He pulled Martin's knife from inside his coat, the one Martin had used in his attempt to kill Carlos, and held it for the quaking man to see. "Poetic justice, is it not?" Carlos said quietly. "To die with your own knife imbedded in your throat?"

Martin squealed with terror. His pale eyes grew huge as the silver blade glinted in the half light.

Chris tugged on the tall vampire's arm again. "Carlos, he's not worth it. Just make him forget all about us, and let's get out of here."

Carlos nodded. "Consider yourself lucky tonight, hunter. Christopher has saved your worthless life." He fixed Martin with another riveting stare then, after a moment, he let the terrified man fall to the floor where he lay in a crumpled heap.

"Not your average fearless vampire hunter," Roger remarked through his laughter.

"Don't think he'll be doing much hunting in the future," Micah said. He looked over at Chris. "So, you all right after all this?"

Chris nodded. "I think so—though I feel like I'll wake up any minute and find this was all just a dream." He gazed up into Carlos' eyes. "And I hope like hell it isn't."

"Well..." Marcus chuckled and put his hand on Roger's shoulder. "I think our work here is done. I suggest we go home and enjoy some wine and each other's company." Chris gaped open mouthed as Marcus and Roger rose into the air, hand in hand, disappearing through the hole torn into the roof, followed a second later by Joseph and Micah.

Carlos smiled at Chris' amazement. "Are you ready for this?" he asked, drawing Chris into his arms.

Chris wound his arms around Carlos' neck, kissing him long and hard. "With you, I'm ready for anything." He felt himself secured in a tight embrace, then, slowly at first, they rose into the air, leaving Martin to gaze upwards at them with uncomprehending eyes.

The night breeze was cool against Chris' bare skin, and when he dared to open his eyes, he saw the lights of Los Angeles beneath him as he and Carlos glided over the city towards the hills. Despite everything he had witnessed in the past hour or so, all of it still seemed totally unbelievable, like it belonged in a dream, but Chris knew he wasn't dreaming. The press of Carlos' powerful body on his, the strong arms wrapped around him was all the proof he needed to know he was wide awake, and that knowledge filled him with an elation he had never before experienced.

"Can we go to my place first?" he shouted above the rushing of wind around them. "I need to get dressed."

Carlos pressed his lips to Chris' ear. "If we do that, we might not make it to our friends' house."

Chris turned to grin at him. "That would be all right, too."

Chapter Seventeen

Once safely inside Chris' apartment, they lost no time in making for the bedroom. But once there, Carlos surprised Chris by taking a robe from the closet and wrapping it around Chris' almost naked body.

"So you won't distract me while we talk," Carlos said with a gentle smile.

"But I want to distract you," Chris protested, trying to shuck off the robe. Carlos held it firmly in place then bent his head to kiss Chris lightly on his lips.

"There are things you should know before we go further."

"I think I just found out the most important thing about you," Chris said, gazing into the golden-brown depths of Carlos' eyes and feeling a visceral thrill in the pit of his stomach.

"And you are not afraid?"

"Of you?" Chris hesitated. "I was. I remember being afraid when you first told me, but now, what I'm more afraid of is losing you or of not remembering you. These past few days seemed empty. I knew I was missing something. I just didn't know what it was." He reached up to touch Carlos' face. "And now, I know it was you and the times we spent together, how happy I was, and how much I loved you. Still love you. You're not going to take that away from me again, are you?"

"Not unless you wish it."

"I don't!"

Carlos cupped Chris' face in his hands and kissed him again gently. "You must understand there will be difficulties ahead of us. Your friends and your parents cannot be told of what I am."

Chris nodded. "I understand. I just don't want to lose you, Carlos." He paused for a moment, thinking. "Am I right in guessing that Ron, the guy who runs that Italian restaurant, isn't a vampire?"

"You are correct." Carlos sat on the bed next to Chris and drew him into his arms. "Ron is still mortal. My cousin's lover Tony is also mortal—although to be honest, I feel there is a need for him to accept the change soon."

"Why?"

"He has been with Andorra a long time. A very long time. Longer than I can remember any mortal surviving the passage of time without the change."

"How long?"

"Over one hundred years."

Chris' eyes grew big as he stared at Carlos. "How...how old are you?"

"I was born in the seventeenth century."

"Oh, wow." Chris remembered a remark Roger had made in the restaurant the night he'd first met Carlos' friends. About Marcus and Joseph being older than God. He'd thought it strange then, and now—

"Marcus was a Roman centurion," Carlos said, answering Chris' unspoken question.

"And you can read my mind, too."

"Yes."

"So Ron will have to change eventually?"

"If he wishes to remain with Jean-Claude, then yes. But there are many more years before he must make that decision."

"How did you become a vampire?"

"By foolishly not listening to my cousin Andorra's warning." Quickly, Carlos related the events that had changed his life forever.

Chris listened with a sense of awe. Yes, there were hundreds more questions he had, and he didn't doubt that some of the answers would leave his mind reeling. But the most incredible part of all this was the fact that Carlos was here with him, holding him in his arms, the chance of their love renewed, and that was what mattered more than anything else. He loved this man, regardless of what he was or the difficulties they would have to face. If he faltered now, if he showed indecision he might lose him again, and that he couldn't bear.

He pressed himself against Carlos' hard chest and slipped a hand inside his vampire lover's shirt, his fingers gliding over the cool, smooth skin, teasing gently at the stiffening nipples.

"I love you, Carlos," he said quietly. "I know there are going to be 'Oh, my God' moments in our lives—

maybe some pretty gigantic ones—but I'm willing to risk it all for you, if you are." He reached up to kiss Carlos' chin. "Maybe Ron can give me some pointers," he added, smiling.

Carlos stroked Chris' face then took his lips in a kiss that was no longer gentle and left Chris gasping for air, filled with a hungry desire that both startled and exhilarated him. He pushed himself deeper into Carlos' embrace, returning his kiss with equal intensity, then stood and, throwing aside his robe, straddled Carlos' thighs.

"Time to make up for what we've missed," he murmured. His eyes widened when, as if by magic, Carlos' clothes disappeared, exposing his perfectly sculpted body to Chris' lustful gaze. "You can do that? Of course, you can. Is there anything you can't do?" he asked, caressing Carlos' chest then lowering his head to take each nipple into his mouth, scouring each hard nub with his teeth and tongue.

Carlos writhed beneath him. "Yes. I can't resist you." He pulled Chris into his arms and rolled him over onto his back. He smiled down into Chris' eyes. "Not that I would ever want to."

He slid his hand down Chris' torso until he reached the throbbing erection that jutted proudly from its nest of golden hair. Chris moaned softly, gazing yet again with love and admiration at the beautiful face that hovered over him. He reached up to slip his hands through the thick black hair that crowned Carlos' head, to draw him nearer, to touch those luscious lips with his own, to hold them pressed to his in a long, lingering kiss. He wound his legs around Carlos' slim waist, raising his hips until he felt the length of hard throbbing flesh pressing into the cleft between his butt cheeks.

Condom, he thought.

There is no need. The words entered his mind as clearly as if Carlos had said them aloud.

"What?" he gasped.

Carlos smiled into his eyes and kissed his lips. "Now that there are no secrets between us, you have no need of protection. We carry no human diseases."

"Wow. I've never done it without…you know. I can't imagine what it would feel like."

"Would you like to find out?"

"You bet. Let me get the lube."

"I can take care of that, too." Carlos inserted one then two fingers into his mouth, slowly coating them with his saliva. Watching this sensual act was almost enough to send Chris over the edge. His cock jumped in anticipation, and as Carlos slid his fingers inside him, Chris pulled him down for another long, searing kiss. He flinched just a little when he felt the head of Carlos' cock nudge at his opening. It was a lot thicker than two fingers.

"Te quiero, querido…"

The words whispered in Chris' ear caused his heart to turn over. His breath hissed through his teeth as Carlos pushed forward, driving his rock-hard erection deep inside Chris, filling him completely. Chris wrapped his arms around Carlos' neck, bringing their mouths together in yet another rapturous kiss while their bodies rocked together and Carlos fucked Chris with long, intensely pleasurable strokes.

This was even more fantastic than Chris had ever thought it could be. To feel, for the first time, his lover's naked flesh deep inside him was an experience so exquisite, Chris knew he would never forget this first glorious time.

His hands slid down the length of Carlos' smooth, muscular back, cupping the round swell of his buttocks, letting his fingers stray into the moist cleft, probing gently at his opening before slipping his middle finger all the way in. Carlos growled as his sweet spot was touched and caressed, and Chris smiled with satisfaction knowing he had brought his lover some of the same powerful sensations that coursed through his own body.

Their rhythm increased, their bodies rocking together in complete unison, Carlos' cock plunging in and out of Chris with a desperate fervour that should have caused pain, but instead brought him an ecstasy incredibly sweet and amazingly raw at the same time. Passion overwhelmed him. He clung to Carlos, thrusting his body up as Carlos bore down, the two of them fused as one, bodies and souls meshed together, neither man willing for this time together to ever end. Chris' eyes met his lover's, now dark with a hungry desire.

"Yes," he gasped, "take me now, Carlos. Make me yours forever."

"*Querido…*"

He shuddered as Carlos laved his neck with his lips and tongue. The sharp prick of fangs on his skin made Chris flinch, but he arched his neck, giving himself willingly to the vampire's kiss.

What more fantastic union could there be than this? he wondered, moaning softly as the initial burning pain receded, replaced by a sensuous yearning so intense it was almost unbearable. To be bound to this incredible man, not only by their flesh, but now by their blood was something that even in his wildest imaginings, he could never have thought possible. As he felt the tug of Carlos' lips against his neck, he tightened his arms and legs about Carlos' torso and pushed his hips higher to take Carlos even deeper inside him. His orgasm roiled in his groin, uncontrollable now as what felt like liquid fire exploded through his blood. He shouted Carlos' name as he came in long, shuddering spasms, a kaleidoscope of stars blossoming behind his closed eyes.

Chris' exhilaration was compounded when Carlos' powerful body stiffened in his arms, and he came, a hoarse cry escaping his lips, and for the first time, Chris experienced the thrill of having his lover's hot semen surge inside him with a searing blast. Chris reared up into Carlos' arms, and his lover held him fast in a bone-crushing embrace, both men now totally intoxicated by what had passed between them.

"So beautiful," Carlos murmured as their bodies calmed. He brushed Chris' hair back from his damp forehead and kissed his lips tenderly. Chris smiled up at him and wriggled his butt around Carlos' still-hard cock, keeping it inside him.

"Beautiful is right," Chris sighed. His eyes glinted. "Am I a vampire now?"

Carlos chuckled softly. "No. Unlike in a movie, one bite does not a vampire make."

"It didn't hurt so very much. Did you get enough to keep you going?"

Carlos chuckled again. "Keep me going?"

Chris blushed. "Well, you know. Don't you have to…uh…have some every day?"

"Not every day." He kissed Chris' nose lightly. "In due course, we will talk of all you must know. Right now, let us enjoy one another's company."

"Does that mean we don't have to go out?"

"Not if you don't want to."

"I'd rather stay here with you. Do you think Marcus and Roger will mind?"

Carlos traced the outline of Chris' lips with his thumb. "I am fairly certain they will not mind at all."

"Good." Chris locked eyes with Carlos. "Don't pinch me. I never want to wake up from this incredible dream."

"Nor do I, *querido*." Carlos smiled. "I have longed for this moment between us, when you would know me for what I am, and not be afraid of me."

"I can't imagine why I ever was afraid of you." Chris ran a fingertip caress down the length of Carlos' strong jaw. "I look at you, and all I see is the most wonderful man I have ever known." Shyly he added, "Once you joked about me getting tired of you 'hanging around', and I said I would never tire of you, even if I lived forever. Now that that's a possibility, I want you to know, I mean it more than ever. *Te quiero*, Carlos."

"*Querido*," Carlos murmured. "*Te amaré para siempre*, I will love you always — until the end of time."

About the Author

J.P. Bowie was born in Scotland and toured British theatres in numerous musical shows including Stephen Sondheim's Company.

Emigrated to the States and worked in Las Vegas, Nevada for the magicians Siegfried and Roy as their Head of Wardrobe at the Mirage Hotel. Currently living in Henderson, Nevada.

J.P. loves to hear from readers. You can find her contact information, website details and author profile page at http://www.total-e-bound.com

Total-E-Bound Publishing

www.total-e-bound.com

Take a look at our exciting range of literagasmic™
erotic romance titles and discover pure quality
at Total-E-Bound.